CREATION SCIENCE CLUB

The Secret of Mission T-3

John and Lisa Fox

The Secret of Mission T-3
The Creation Science Club: Book 5
by John and Lisa Fox

First printing: January 2016

ISBN 978-1-942773-04-7
Cover design: BookFuel
Design and layout: BookFuel
Style and proofreading: Dr. Robert Carter and Lita Cosner

Published by:

CREATION
BOOK PUBLISHERS

Creation Book Publishers
P.O. Box 350
Powder Springs, GA, 30127, USA.
Phone: 1-800-616-1264
creationbookpublishers.com

We dedicate this book to
John's parents, Tom and Susan,
for their lives of love and service
in the name of Jesus Christ.

We also want to thank:

Buddy Davis, whose creation music ministry and dinosaur sculpting first inspired us to dig deeper into the truth,

Jonathan Sarfati, who has written books to refute the endless barrage of evolution's 'overwhelming evidence' coming at us from every side,

Creation Ministries International, for providing us all with various resources and an endless supply of 'scientific stones of truth' for our slings.

With special gratitude to Dr. Robert Carter, Lita Cosner, and others at CMI for taking the time to review this book.

*Note: If any errors or misuse of terms or facts
occur in this series, these mistakes are solely
the responsibility of the authors.

CHAPTER 1

The end seemed near. Dufthak backed himself against the ship's mast as he watched his captain fall to the merciless strength of the mighty sea serpent. The deck of the *Scandinavian* was already strewn with the bodies of those who had given their lives in an effort to save the ship: Arngrim, the ship's first mate; Alrek, who had been Dufthak's closest friend; and now, Captain Joekull himself.

These brave sailors, however, had not gone down without leaving their mark on the beast. Deep gashes on the neck and head of the Jormangund oozed its cold black blood. And now, it eyed the cutlass in Dufthak's hand with a wary hesitancy.

Dufthak was no hero, but he knew he could not allow the Jormangund to live. It must not be left to heal and then return to terrorize other hapless sailors. Seeing that the serpent was hesitant to attack, Dufthak taunted, "You aren't so mighty after all. Would you defeat the ship's captain and then run from the ship's cook!"

Opening its gaping mouth with a hiss, the beast prepared to answer. But a strange sound caught its attention. Dufthak heard it as well. What was it? He had heard the sound before. It sounded like a giggle—like a little girl's giggle.

With a blush, Dufthak quickly lowered his cutlass. The Jormangund pulled its tongue back into its mouth and lowered itself to the ship's deck. Then it slithered over to peek behind one of the ship's lifeboat covers. Captain Joekull, Alrek, and Arngrim all quickly 'resurrected' and joined Dufthak and the giant serpent by the lifeboat.

Hiding behind the canvas cover was a dark-eyed, dark-haired girl. The Jormangund smiled and said, "Well, hello there. Who are you?"

Jack (Captain Joekull) had conscientiously pulled off his *Reality Morphing* glasses but also had a grin for the stranger. "Hey," he teased, "were you spying on us?"

The girl looked embarrassed at being caught. But her dimples got the best of her, and she came out of her hiding place with a laugh. "You guys are so funny! What on earth were you doing?"

Aaron (Alrek) explained with dignity, "We were doing battle with the mighty Jormangund of the Norse seas."

David (Dufthak) slipped his *R.M.* glasses onto the girl and told her to look at Darin. Suddenly, Darin was a huge sea serpent suspended 20 feet above the ship's deck on a snake-like body. The girl took several quick steps backward, then peeked over the top of the glasses for a re-check with reality. "Whoa, that is so…totally awesome! You'll have to let my brother see these. Please?" The girl turned imploringly to Darin.

"I don't see why not," Abel (Arngrim) responded. "So, who are you, anyway? And, who's your brother?"

Flashing her dimples again, the girl answered, "I'm Sarah Chen, and I'm eight. My brother's name is Mark, and he's 12. We're on the ship with our father. He's a scientist who's going to study the wildlife on some of the islands in Glacier Bay. Our mother is in California taking care of our sick grandmother."

"Oh, yeah," Jack said as they walked toward some steps leading to a lower deck on the ship. "I remember Billy saying that a Dr. Chen was going to be on board. He's kind of famous, isn't he?"

Sarah giggled, "I guess so. Anyway, he's super smart."

"Well," David said, "my name's David Avila. My dad's a pastor. My whole family is on the ship. We're using the time to plan the opening of a Creation Museum in our town."

"Oh, I see," Sarah said. "So, what's a *Creation Museum*?"

"I'm Jack Hill," a nearly 14-year-old boy with lots of summer freckles jumped in. "My twin sister and my uncle are on board. My uncle's a scientist, too. Anyway, a Creation Museum has lots of evidence in it showing that God created the world in six days, instead of the world creating itself in billions of years."

"Oh, I see," Sarah said again.

"I'm Aaron Franklin," said a tall African-American of 14 with a handsome smile. "My sister, Tasha, is on board, too. She's 16. We're all part of the Creation Science Club."

"Oh, I see, the Creation Science Club…" Sarah looked impressed. "What's that?"

One of the two older boys in the group answered, "I'm Darin Tadue, and this strange-looking fellow, here, is my twin brother Abel—a.k.a. Arngrim." After patting his identical twin on the back, Darin continued, "And, about four years ago, a great guy—Billy James—and his wife took on the challenge of a lifetime—lookin' after Abel and me.

"Turns out, we were a great match. So, together, we decided to start some sort of a club that would show the world that the Bible can be trusted from the very first verse."

"Then," David spoke up, "at the beginning of this past school year, Billy, Abel, and Darin volunteered as tutors at my middle school. Just like them, I wanted to face and fight evolution, so I joined their Club. Later, Jack, Aaron, and the girls joined, too."

"Oh, I see," Sarah said once again. "My dad talks about evolution all the time. Does that mean that he's wrong?"

All the boys were quiet for a moment, then Abel spoke up, "Well, I think it'd be best if we met your dad and talked to him before we say whether he's right or wrong. I'm sure there'll be lots of time to talk about it all while we're on the ship together."

"Yeah," Aaron agreed. "Wasn't it great luck that the *Scandinavian*'s owners wanted to test her out on Glacier Bay before her first real voyage at the end of the month?"

"I'm glad you guys are here," Sarah said decidedly. "I can tell things are going to be a lot more fun with all of you around."

****

Half an hour later, the ever-growing Creation Science Club was up on deck with Dr. Chen and his two children. Billy stared off into the massive wilderness with his arm around his wife, Carmen. Darin and Bekah Soure had a fast-paced contest to see who could name the most landmarks as they sailed along the Icy Strait. Big Auger and Stego Soure were talking fishing tackle.

Suddenly, Abel hopped up, grabbed Natasha (Aaron's big sister) by the arm and pulled her toward the ship's railing. "Look alive!" he called out in the weathered old voice of a sea captain as he pointed out toward the cold waters. "Yonder! She's 'bout ta go…aha! Thar she blows!"

About 40 yards away the waters churned, then a misty spout sprayed some 15 feet into the air. A dark form broke the surface, then the huge creature arched its back and dived. Before it disappeared, it seemed to wave to them with its large white tail flukes.

Everyone stood transfixed by the railing. "Super-fan-taz-cool-o-rama!" Darin said with awe. "A real live humpback whale!"

Then, most everyone scattered in a quick race to get their binoculars and cameras before the whale left the area.

When a second whale surfaced even closer to the ship, Billy commented to Dr. Chen, "Can't help but think of poor old Jonah every time I see one of those big beautiful critters."

Dr. Chen smiled, but shook his head. "You don't really think that old story's true, do you?"

Billy smiled back but spoke seriously. "Of course I do! Why would God put it in the Bible if we weren't supposed to believe it? Besides, Jesus believed it was true. He even spoke of Jonah's three days in the fish as a sign of His own three days in the tomb before His resurrection."

Dr. Chen looked quite taken back. "I…I never thought of it that way. I just thought it was one of those Bible stories we were supposed to learn a lesson from. You know, like Adam and Eve and Noah's Ark and things."

Billy watched the tail of one of the whales disappear beneath the water, then answered, "Jesus also talked about Adam and Eve, and about the times of Noah. He spoke of them as fact, real history, not just stories with good lessons."

Dr. Chen again looked surprised. He was about to respond, but one of the whales came up so close to the ship that everyone stopped talking and just watched in utter amazement as the whales seemed to perform just for their audience's enjoyment.

****

"David," Billy called across the medium-sized dinghy. "I'm gonna need you to pull on that oar with Aaron. The water's getting pretty choppy, and we need to get closer to the shore."

David quickly joined Aaron on the right oar while Billy worked the left, and Tasha guarded the equipment from the splashing water. Dr. Chen and Darin had already landed their dinghy. So, as soon as the second one was close enough, Darin threw Tasha a rope to help pull them to shore.

On shore, Sarah shivered up close to her dad, and David and Mark turned their backs to the cold winds that came off the bay. "Hmmm, the weather seems to have taken an unexpected turn," Dr. Chen remarked as they secured the rubber rafts.

Billy looked at the skies around the island, then told Darin, "You'd better hail the *Scandinavian* and request weather information every half hour."

"Aye-Aye, Sir!" Darin answered, using his specially designed wristband to contact the ship's crew.

"Anyway, Dad," Mark said, "South Marble is your last island."

"Yep." Dr. Chen smiled and turned to Billy. "Things have gone a lot quicker with your gang along. I doubt I could have even finished the first two islands on my own, but with your help, I've gotten to four."

Billy laughed. "Really, I'm the one who should be thanking you. Sitting in meetings all day—even on a cruise ship—is *not* my idea of fun. Give me the ocean and uninhabited islands any day."

As the group climbed up and over the wet and rocky area along the shore, Tasha pulled her coat hood tighter around her face. "Gee, it wouldn't be so bad if there wasn't so much wind."

"You can be thankful for this wind," Dr. Chen told her. "Summer-time in these parts is mosquito season. And Alaskan mosquitoes show no mercy."

As the group climbed higher, Dr. Chen pointed to a large group of Steller sea lions pulled out onto a smoother part of the small crescent-shaped island. “Looks like those guys are preparing for a storm. Notice how many are pulled out. And look, they’re pretty far inland,” he added with a note of concern.

“The ship said the weather radar shows rain,” Darin informed them. “But, then, it’s rained every day—except for the first day—of this trip.”

“This is hard weather on the nesting birds,” Dr. Chen commented. “The rainy season doesn’t usually hit this hard for several more weeks.”

As the group topped a rocky hill, Dr. Chen sent out the predetermined search teams. Billy, Tasha, and Sarah ran one direction, while Darin, David, and Aaron ran another. Dr. Chen stayed on a flat rock with Mark and began preparing to receive data.

About 20 minutes later, Sarah was back by her father’s side. “Daddy,” she said all warmed up by her hiking over the rough terrain, “we found a gulls’ nesting site. Billy says there’s 80 nests or more.”

As Dr. Chen stood up to follow his daughter, a wind-whipped drizzle began to fall. He pressed his wristband and called to Darin’s group, “Hey, Darin, can you three come over with us to this nest site? I’m gonna need everyone’s eyes to get as much data as possible before the hard rain hits. Then, we’ll need to take cover until it’s over.”

Once everyone had reached the nesting site, they all spread out around the glaucous-winged gulls, trying not to disturb them as they tended their nests. Dr. Chen sat under a dry ledge logging all the information his assistants were sending him over their wristbands.

When Billy finished his area, he came over to Dr. Chen with a serious expression. “D’you notice all the birds are landing? Even some of the rafts of waterfowl are coming inland.”

Dr. Chen looked up in surprise. “Oh my! I’m afraid I was so wrapped up in the data collection that I wasn’t watching. Why don’t you go ahead and find a suitable shelter while the others finish up.”

As Billy headed off, the wind shifted, and the temperature seemed to instantly drop 20 degrees. Everyone pulled their hoods back up and gathered quickly by Dr. Chen as he zipped his computer into a waterproof case. The rain changed from a drizzle to large, heavy drops. They all huddled under Dr. Chen’s little ledge until Billy whistled to them from somewhere above. Then, with Billy in the lead, and Dr. Chen and Darin taking up the rear, they all scurried higher up the mountainous little island.

Everyone shook the big drops of rain off their coats as they entered the dark cave. Billy and Darin pulled out their flashlights and set them up to light the small cave while Dr. Chen tried to hail the ship near the entrance. “There must be too much rock between us and them,” he concluded. “I can’t reach them.”

Suddenly, any light from the cave entrance seemed to disappear. “Wow!” Billy said, “This is a real doozy of a storm. I can’t even see four feet out into that rain.”

Dr. Chen paced the small cave and fretted, “This will be really hard on the nesting birds.”

Sarah came over and held her father’s hand. “Don’t worry, Daddy. God will take care of the birds.” Dr. Chen smiled but still looked worried.

In a rush, Mark ran up to his father. His eyes were wide with uncertain adventure. “Hey, Dad, you’ve got to come and see what David and I found in the back of the cave. It looks like a human skeleton.”

The group tingled with fearful excitement as they followed Mark to a sort of small cave within the cave. Sarah and Tasha, however, hung back, feeling a bit creeped out.

David had crawled into the small 'closet' and was shining his flashlight onto the skeleton.

"I'll bet it was some sort of prehistoric caveman," Mark exclaimed. "Maybe a Neanderthal or something. What do you think, Dad?"

Dr. Chen shook his head. "I'm afraid if it's not a bird, I'm not going to be much help."

So, Billy got down and crawled forward. David squeezed out past him and handed him the flashlight. Then, Billy crawled further in and examined the skeleton and the area around it. In a minute, he backed his way out and handed Mark a small object.

"A ring," David said, looking into Mark's hand.

"That's right," Billy nodded. "It's a wedding ring—from the ring finger of his left hand. That pretty much rules out Neanderthals. However, from what I could see, this poor fellow has been here for quite some time. He must have been a hunter or explorer from when the glacier first receded enough to open up the Bay. And, by the way he's positioned and from the lack of personal items, I'd say he died a while before he was washed into this cave. It must have been when the Bay's waters were higher."

"Look!" Tasha exclaimed when it was her turn to look at the ring. "Hey, David, shine your light this way. There's something inscribed on the inside of the ring...*1 John 4:12. Dean & Susi 4-ever.*"

"What's *1 John 4:12* say?" Aaron wondered.

"I know that one," Darin answered from behind the others. "'No one has ever seen God; but if we love one another, God lives in us and his love is made complete in us.'"

"How sweet..." Tasha sighed. "But, how sad..."

Billy took the ring from Tasha and crawled back into the small space to put the ring back on its owner's fleshless finger.

"Aw, man," Mark complained, trying to lighten up the serious mood. "I was hoping to find 'the missing link.' Then we'd all be rich and famous." Everyone chuckled, then headed back toward the front of the cave.

"Billy," Dr. Chen began as they sat down, "I'm guessing from what we've talked about over the last few days that your Club doesn't believe there even is a missing link to be found. If that's true, then how do you explain the existence of Neanderthals and other human ancestors?"

"Well," Billy asked with a smile, "do you want the short answer or the long answer?"

"Oh, oh, oh!" Darin clapped his hands together. "Tell him you want the long answer! Tell him you want the long answer!"

"Okay," Dr. Chen laughed. "Seeing how—thanks to this storm—we seem to have time on our hands, why don't you go ahead and give us the *long answer.*"

"Oh, boy! Oh, boy!" Darin quickly plopped down and rubbed his hands together with delight.

David jabbed Mark with his elbow and said, "Listen up, Billy's the greatest story teller ever."

Tasha settled back against the cave wall and let Sarah curl up against her to get extra comfy-cozy.

Billy looked out into the blank nothingness of the rain falling outside the cave…

CHAPTER 2

Looking out into the blank nothingness of outer space, Dean could once again see Susi's tear-stained face nearly lost in the crowd of well-wishers. It seemed like years ago. But, of course, the price of exploration and discovery was always high. In spite of the risks, Susi had always said she was proud to be married to a 'trail-blazer.'

Dean smiled to himself and absent-mindedly spun the wedding band on his left hand. There weren't many things more trail-blazing than confirming the existence of a new planet hiding behind the sun—unless it were visiting that planet and discovering that it supported life. Wow! What a thought!

However, this mission also held considerable risks. NISA (New International Space Agency) had made it clear to all competing for a place on the Discovery 2's crew that the odds of their returning alive stood at a grim 25%. Dean had been the only married astronaut chosen by NISA—they didn't want to create any widows or orphans.

Closing his eyes briefly, Dean prayed that he would be allowed to return safely in time for his 30th wedding anniversary. Then, with a sigh, he pushed himself back from the window and turned to one of the many on-board experiments his team was in charge of monitoring. Flopsy, Mopsy, and Cotton-Tail were all imminently due to kindle their litters. They would be the first mammals born on a spacecraft as it orbited around the sun.

"Hey, Chief!" a broad-built, handsome black man ducked into what they called the *Zoo*. It was the largest room on the ship—the room designated to house all the mammals on board, including the humans. Leaning over the separate rabbit cages, John poked a finger into one of them. Mopsy hopped over to let him scratch her between the ears. "I've got a piece of NISA's 'famous' key lime cheesecake riding on Mopsy, here, going first. Dave's sure it'll be Cotton-Tail."

Dean smiled but shook his head. "You know everyone is supposed to eat exactly what NISA has on the menu. No begging, borrowing, or stealing."

"Yeah, yeah," John rolled his eyes and turned to leave. "But since we're about 100 million miles from Earth, I don't think one dessert is going to make much of a difference to NISA."

Dean sighed again. Everyone seemed a little on edge today.

As John ducked back into the *Aviary*, he was greeted by a blue and yellow macaw. "The king is a fink!" it screeched. John had to laugh, but still felt pretty down. He had spent two years studying, working-out, and praying for God to help him beat out all the competition. And, he had won. Here he was, the one black man chosen out of more than 500 applicants. It had all seemed so exciting, so glamorous—the parade, the presidential speech, the medals...But, now, it just seemed like what it was—a long and dangerous mission to a destination that might not even exist.

Flipping open a small computer, John began inputting data from the *Aviary*. The larger birds seemed to be adjusting well to space travel. However, the smaller birds didn't seem so happy.

A wide, round face appeared in the door. Joe, the mission's Asian member, entered the *Aviary* with a pooch close at his heels. John closed up his computer and reached out to greet everyone's favorite crewmember—a 3-year-old mini Golden Doodle named Laika. "Looks like the red tulip is going to bloom tomorrow," Joe said in a tone of satisfaction.

After he was done getting his face washed by Laika, John asked casually, "Did Dave's python ever lay her eggs?"

"Yep," Joe said as he sat down and opened up a NISA-ordered protein bar. "Six of 'em. But he's been having trouble with his hissing cockroaches today. Something seems to be disturbing their normal activities."

"Really?" Dean asked stepping out of the Zoo and into the *Aviary*. "I've noticed my shrews aren't eating like they should be today."

"Hmmm..." Joe pondered, looking at his uneaten protein bar. "I'll have to say, I don't feel much like eating myself."

As if on cue, Dave (the team's European member) stepped into the now crowded *Aviary* and said, "Hey, I'm not feeling too good, guys. I think I'm gonna lie down for half an hour and see what comes of it. I want to be ready before we reach the halfway mark and begin deceleration." But, before he could get to the Zoo, he stopped and clutched at his stomach. Then, suddenly, everyone bent forward—gasping in pain. The parrots were screeching, and Laika was yelping. And then...

****

"Better scoot on out while the rain's at half-pace, Darin."

Darin blinked several times and gave a confused grunt, "Huh?"

Billy cleared his throat. "I said, you'd better scoot on out and try to contact the *Scandinavian* while the rain has slowed a bit."

"Oh, yeah, okay," Darin said, pulling up his hood. "David and Aaron, I'm trusting you two to make sure he doesn't tell even one word of the story until I'm back." Then he disappeared into the slacking rain.

"Why did everyone get sick?" Mark asked, as soon as Darin was gone.

"I can't tell," Billy laughed. "Darin wouldn't forgive me."

"Well, Billy," Dr. Chen said, "at least tell us what four men in a spaceship full of animals has to do with Neanderthal man?"

"You'll see," Billy teased. "You're the one that asked for the *long version*." Then Billy looked out at the rain. "Did you all know that in the late 1700s, Glacier Bay was under a mile thick sheet of ice all the way out to Icy Strait?"

"A *mile*?" Sarah gasped. "That's really thick!"

"That's right," Dr. Chen said. "But, once it decided to melt, it didn't take too long. By the late 1800s, more than 30 miles of the glacier ice had already retreated. Then, by 1960, it had retreated 60 miles, opening up Glacier Bay and forming the very islands we've been doing my research on this week."

"That's pretty cool!" David sat forward. "Like, that means this island was under a mile of ice when Thomas Jefferson wrote the Declaration of Independence."

"Yep," Dr. Chen nodded. "And still under ice during the Civil War. You see, Glacier Bay is a brand new creation. As the ice melted back, it left a barren, lifeless land. But, with the sun, soon small plants began to grow in the fertile soil dropped by the glacier ice. Then, with the plants came the bugs, then more plants, then birds…It's all really fascinating—a biologist's dream. We get to literally watch life repopulate a once lifeless land."

"Hey!" Aaron complained as Darin ducked back into the cave. "You're getting me all wet!"

Darin ignored him and sat down, saying all in one breath, "I contacted the ship. They know we're safe. Now, go on with the story."

****

Joe was the first to wake up, with Laika whimpering and licking his face. As soon as his head was clear, he reached over to shake John. Soon, all the men were up, feeling shaky, but fine.

"Aw, John, look at your birds," Dean said in a hushed tone.

Looking around the *Aviary*, John took in the loss. Nothing smaller than a robin had made it. He had lost nearly 75% of his birds.

Dean then turned quickly toward the Zoo, while Dave headed toward the Critter Room, and Joe to the Gardens.

Ten minutes later, they met in the Zoo and reported their losses after the 'black-out.' No caged insects had survived, but the fish seemed unaffected. The shrews were back to eating, but the gerbils were dead. Flopsy had also died—seemingly of fright. The plants were fine. And, interestingly, the insects native to the tropical plants had survived. But, the insects on the desert plants were dead.

They couldn't figure out what had happened during the shift to the deceleration phase of the trip, or why. It was an unsettling mystery.

After a while, they each headed toward their own labs to document the phenomenon and its resulting data in their personal logs. This would be important information that must make it back to Earth, even if nothing else, or no one else, did.

****

"Land ho!" Dean's voice came through the ship's speakers. Joe, John, and Dave all ran to the Zoo and crowded around the ship's largest window. There, before them, was the answer to one of NISA's biggest questions: Does T-3 really exist? Now, the crew of the Discovery 2 knew the answer—*Yes!*

"Yo, Dave," John said, "looks like I win this one. If we ever make it back home, you owe me a Biggie Burgers Double Deluxe Meal Deal."

"No way!" Dave smirked. "I knew it was there all along, I was just playing along to keep things interesting."

"Yeah, right!" John rolled his eyes. "Anyway, I've got it all in my journal."

Joe spoke up. "Well, make sure you write down in your journal that you owe me a double dip of Favorite Flavors supreme wildberry ice cream, seeing that I got my Christmas cactus to bloom." Joe was a real ice cream connoisseur.

"That's hardly fair!" John complained. "Man, you can get anything to bloom."

"Hey!" Joe shook his head. "You made the bet, not me!"

"Okay then," John said, "how about double or nothing on whether there's life on T-3?"

"I bet we find clear evidence of microscopic life," Dave said.

"Well," Joe said, "I'm willing to bet we find life forms evolving like we've never seen on Earth."

"Whoa! But, what if we, like, find life forms that are even more advanced than we are?" Dave wondered.

"Yeah, right," John scoffed. "Maybe they've already been visiting us back on Earth. Dude, you've been watchin' too many old movies."

Amid the continuing debates, Dean just stared out at the ever-growing planet before them. "Well, Susi, looks like you were right. It has been worth the trip."

****

After orbiting for three days around T-3, the crew couldn't believe what they were seeing. After decades of space exploration, science had finally found a planet similar to Earth, a planet that might possibly even support life. Who would have thought that all of that looking out light-years into space would have led us back to our own solar system—to a planet that had been hiding behind the sun—on a parallel orbit to Earth? But here it really was, being seen for the very first time.

Discovery 2 came to rest on the surface of the newly discovered planet without incident. In some ways, the terrain around them was very similar to their own Earth—with brown dirt, green plants, and clear signs of water. Yet, it was different—especially the sky—it seemed darker, hazier, even when the sun was out. And, would there be animal life?

From inside their ship, the crew immediately went to work gathering all sorts of data. Four robotic explorers moved around the immediate area collecting photos and air and dirt samples. This information would be stored in the pod the crew would send into orbit around T-3 before leaving the safety of the ship. That way, the data would be retrievable by NISA, even if the crewmembers were lost.

Forty-eight hours after landing, Joe climbed down the ship's ladder. Seven video cameras documented the event from all angles. Once on the ground, Joe cautiously began to remove his protective gear—one piece at a time. His crewmates played silly music and cheered him on through the ship's outer speakers.

Finally, Joe stood on the surface of the newly discovered planet wearing nothing more than what any normal earthling would wear on a mild winter's day. Gathering all the gear he had stripped off, Joe stored it in one of the ship's outer compartments. Then, he turned to wave to his friends. "Come on down," he called, "the 'water's' fine!"

With a hoot and a holler, Dave, John, and Dean scrambled down the ladder onto the surface of T-3.

"Wow," John said in awe, "those scientists from the institute were right. This *is* Earth's twin sister."

"It's, like, too wild," Dave said, walking over to look at a nearby bush. "If we hadn't just traveled halfway around the sun, I'd say we'd just landed back on Earth—somewhere in Canada—maybe near Alaska."

"Okay," Dean got down to business. "NISA has us scheduled for a two hour on-foot planetary exploration. We're to stick together, then return to the ship to input all our observations. We'll send off a second pod this evening."

They weren't far from the ship when John called out, "Hey, Chief, looks like there *is* animal life on T-3. Come check out these tracks."

Bending down, Dean—the crew's mammal specialist—fingered the outline of the animal prints. "Looks like some sort of cat, maybe..." Then he pulled down his brows. "He's a big one. But, look at the spread between his paces...He's probably only about as long as a cougar. Hmmm...but, if I compare how deep his prints are compared to ours, I'd say he must weigh close to 400 pounds."

Dave whistled through his teeth, then glanced nervously over his shoulder. "I wasn't planning on meetin' up with no 400 pound cougar thing!"

"Don't worry," Joe said, "if he's anything like the big cats back home, he'll be long gone before we ever get a chance to see him."

"Yeah, right!" John shook his head. "That's what the ranger told me and Dave when we went hikin' in California two years back."

"And, that cougar stalked us for three hours before we finally convinced it to scram," Dave said, looking over his shoulder again.

"Come on, let's get going," Dean said with excitement gleaming in his eyes. "This is more incredible than I could have ever imagined."

****

Soo-sahn pulled the woolly blanket up closer around her as she stirred up the small fire. Tah-hom and Tah-him had been gone for more than a week. They should be home soon. Wah-ulf and Suh-mer had been letting Soo-sahn eat with their family over the last two days. It was good to have another family nearby, even if they weren't of the Cle-ahn-tur clan. Winter would come soon enough. Together, maybe they could gather enough food to store for the blizzard season.

Little Tah-hommy stopped looking out of the cave entrance and snuggled close to Soo-sahn. "Momma, I'm bored. Jah-hon promised to teach me how to make a spearhead today."

Soo-sahn ruffled her son's tangled hair and answered, "Well, he promised he'd chip me out a new knife so that I can cut this mane of yours off." Then, she laughed. "I can't imagine what your father and brother are going to look like when they get home from their hunting trip."

"I bet they sure will smell bad," Tah-hommy said, wrinkling up his nose.

"I don't mind what they smell like, as long as they bring home some meat," Soo-sahn said as she stood up and walked out of the cave to get some more wood for the fire. The sun was warm, and Soo-sahn let it sink in for a minute. Down below, she saw two of her sons, Jah-hon and Jah-him, climbing quickly up toward the cave. She waved to them, then started back to the cave without taking any branches from the woodpile. It was good to have sons.

Jah-him didn't even glance at the woodpile as he ran toward the cave, but Jah-hon stopped to gather up an armload of wood. "Momma! Tah-hommy!" Jah-him spread his arms wide in excitement. "You'll never believe what we saw."

"A tail-banger?" Tah-hommy guessed with wide eyes.

"Nope." Jah-him smiled at his little brother.

"A knife-cat?" Tah-hommy guessed again. Soo-sahn turned toward her Jah-him with a worried look.

"No, no." Jah-him shook his head. "Don't worry, Momma, that cat's been scared of us ever since Jah-hon speared him in the rear when he came after our meat." Jah-him paused, then burst out, "Jah-hon and I saw a star, a real big star up in the sky."

Soo-sahn stopped poking at the fire and looked up in surprise, then shook her finger at her son. "Come, now, Jah-himmy! You don't see stars in the daytime. You're always making up stories."

"You do when it's the *Lord's star*," Jah-him answered solemnly.

"Jah-him!" Soo-sahn scolded. "Don't you go getting Tah-hommy all excited!"

"What did it look like?" Tah-hommy asked in awe.

"It was big, and shiny, and it seemed to be falling right out of the sky."

Soo-sahn turned to Jah-hon as he came into the cave and dropped his large load of wood against the wall. "Jah-honny, your brother is saying you two saw a star in broad daylight."

Jah-hon bent down and began stacking the wood neatly along the cave wall. "I'm not sure, Mom. We certainly saw something that we've never seen before."

"It was a star. That's the only thing it *could* have been!" Jah-him said emphatically. "It's the *Lord's star*. Great help is on the way, I just know it."

"Jah-him, what kind of help do you mean?" Soo-sahn asked, pulling the blanket back around her. "The Lord continues to give us all that we need," Soo-sahn added as she began to prepare an herbal stew to share with Suh-mer's family. It wasn't much, but she felt they should bring what they could to the joint meal.

Jah-hon bent down to let Tah-hommy climb onto his back. "Mom, you're right. We do have all that we *need*," he said looking around the dark, barren cave. "But, I have a feeling that the Lord can give us a *whole lot more*." Then, he headed out to teach his little brother how to make a spearhead.

****

"Sure wish we could have a fire going in here," Billy said, pulling his gloves back onto his chilled hands. "But, we'd get smoked out before we even got it started, not to mention that there probably isn't a dry piece of wood on the island."

It was a full five seconds before his audience realized Billy had stopped telling the story and was speaking of their present situation.

"Don't stop, Billy," Mark begged. "See, it's still raining hard."

"Who are Soo-sahn and Jah-hon?" Tasha asked.

"What's a 'knife-cat'?" Dr. Chen wanted to know.

"And, what's the Lord's…?" David began.

But, Billy raised his hands with a laugh. "You'll see…"

CHAPTER 3

John had never run so fast in his life. Slipping on the icy mud, he went down hard. His head struck a rock, but adrenaline had him back on his feet before he had time to feel the pain. He had to make it back to his rover.

Earlier that morning, the crew had come to the critical decision to not base their main exploratory research on this area of Planet T-3. It was too cold. While everything was new and exciting in and of itself, they had all agreed that so much more must be waiting to be documented on a warmer part of the planet. They would spend the day gathering as many pictures and samples as possible, then, early tomorrow, they would use their one spare fuel cell to move the ship to a warmer climate.

John had spent a fairly fruitless morning in search of T-3 bird life. He had seen a few larger birds from a distance, but they had flown away before he could zoom in for a good picture.

Then, just before the crew's scheduled lunch break, he had seen brightly colored feathers in one of the low-growing bushes. Zooming his camera to its max, he had taken a picture every step as he got closer to the mystery bird. Then it flew, but only to another bush about 30 feet further away.

Resetting his camera, John had closed in on it. Again it flew. This time, John had been able to get two shots of the bird in flight. He hoped they wouldn't be blurred. It was hard to get a clear distance shot since the flash wouldn't help from so far away. The sun was out, but it just didn't seem to shine as brightly on T-3 as it did on Earth.

With all his concentration focused on the blue and yellow feathers within his viewfinder, he hadn't noticed two pairs of curious eyes following his every move. Soon two noses had begun to twitch. They could smell NISA's turkey and noodles casserole and cherry pie in John's small backpack. Two brown, furry bodies had worked their way cautiously toward the creature with the clicking silver box. When they were about 20 feet away, John had turned toward their snuffling sounds.

"Oh, my!" he said in a very quiet voice. "Aren't you two, ah, big…I think…" he added as he began to slowly back away. "I think I'd like a little—actually, a lot—more distance between us."

The creatures had hesitated at the sound of his voice. John definitely didn't want them any closer, so he kept talking. "You guys look like some sort of bear or something. I'd call you cubs, except that you're bigger than most full-grown bears." After getting 100 feet between them, John had risked a photo of the pair. Then, just as he had begun to relax and enjoy the playful antics of his subjects, there came a crashing in the bushes behind them. Up out of the bushes rose what must have been the biggest bear in the world. On its hind legs, it was at least 13 feet tall. It had looked straight at John, then crashed back onto all fours with a mighty roar.

John dropped his camera and ran for his life.

Now, John jumped into his little one-man rover and floored it. At top speed, the rover would only hit about

40 miles an hour—and that wasn't going to happen on this mushy, half-frozen grassland. John knew that momma bear could probably catch him if she wanted to. "Go, go, go!" he urged the rover as he raced toward the ice sheet. He figured that if he could hit a smooth part of the glacier's edge, he might have the advantage with his high traction wheels.

John had no trouble hearing the huffing growls of the bear behind him, but he didn't dare look back. There were just too many obstacles he had to avoid. Once on the ice, there came a comforting quiet. About 100 yards onto the ice, John peeked back while maintaining his high speed. The momma bear and her cubs were headed back toward the tall brush. "Whew!" John said as he pulled his rover to a stop. "That was *too* close!"

Then, as his heart rate slowed, his head began to throb. Reaching up a hand, John felt a large bump right above his left ear. Just feeling it made him woozy. Reaching down, he grabbed a handful of slushy ice and put it to his head. But, as he turned the rover around to head back to the ship, he realized he didn't know which direction to go. With a frown on his brow, he tried to think. But, it was like his mind refused to give up the information he was looking for. Suddenly, a new kind of fear started to rise up inside of John.

****

Fifty yards up and over from the family's home-cave entrance, Tah-him and Jah-hon finished packing five feet of snow and ice over the 50 pound stash of meat. They marked the place with a thick braid of green reeds.

"Well," Tah-him said with satisfaction, "we're one step closer to not going hungry this coming winter. "Mom is drying another 50 pounds of the hard-back's meat right now. But, we'll need more successful hunts before we will have enough." Heading down the slippery slope with the confidence that comes with practice, Tah-him added, "You just never know how often the blizzards will come."

"Or how long they'll last," Jah-hon added.

In the home cave, the two brothers found Wah-ulf and Suh-mer had come to visit. Wah-ulf and his wife both had long black hair that they always kept in two braids. Jah-hon chose to stay back in the cave shadows. He had met dozens of families during his own family's migrations. But, he had never met anyone that looked like Wah-ulf and his family. He knew they were honest and hardworking people. But, they just looked so different. Everything about them seemed so long and slender. And they lacked something in their faces. Wah-ulf's face seemed all the more different, because he never even had the shadow of a beard. It just wasn't normal. But they did have three nice daughters. The girls looked like their parents, but they didn't speak with their parent's strong accent. John thought that Whin-die was, well, kinda pretty.

Big Tah-hom sat by the fire with little Tah-hommy on his lap. Jah-hon noticed that his mom had put the new knife he had made for her to good use. His father's hair was cut short, and he hardly had a beard. Jah-hon reached up to feel his own lack of a beard. By his age, Tah-him had had to cut his beard twice. Looking down at his own long, slender fingers, Jah-hon hoped that he wouldn't end up looking like the eastern people Wah-ulf's family had come from—long and hairless.

"Jah-hon," Tah-hom called. "Come over here. What we are discussing involves you." Jah-hon went over and sat down between his mother and Jah-him.

"Son," Tah-hom said in a serious tone, "Wah-ulf says he met a family from the west that says there is a large herd of tree-horns a week's walk to the west. We figure if our two families follow the herd for several days, we can kill many. Your mother, Suh-mer, and her girls can come along to cut and dry the meat as we men continue to hunt. That way, we can collect all the meat both our families will need for the winter before the new moon even begins."

"That would be wonderful, Dad!" Jah-hon said. "That way, we could all be home together for the wet weeks of fall." Then, Jah-hon continued excitedly, "I've never been on a long hunt. I'll bet I down the biggest tree-horn of all!"

"No way!" Jah-him smacked his brother's arm. "You watch. My tree-horn will be 10 feet tall, with antlers 11 feet across—just like the one Dad downed last year."

"No, I'm sorry, sons," Big Tah-hom said in a voice that allowed no argument. "Jah-hon, you will remain here with Jah-him and Tah-hommy. It will be your responsibility to watch your brothers and to guard our cave and our meat."

Tah-hommy started to cry, but Jah-hon and Jah-him simply answered, "Okay, Dad." They had long been taught to honor their parents—it was clearly the will of the Lord.

****

Bending over, Joe picked up the camera John had dropped as he ran from the giant bear. Dean was reading the story all the tracks had to tell. "Looks like John was studying something in the area. See, his tracks leading up to here show he was walking slowly, and stopping frequently.

"But, then, look here. It looks like he saw something that made him back up pretty quickly. I'd guess it's whatever made these paw prints. There's a bunch right around there. Looks like two big bears. But, these guys are *nothing* compared to whatever it was that came charging out of the bushes. It must have been some sort of monster bear."

Dean, Joe, and Dave had begun their search for John soon after lunch. They had all agreed that morning to meet back at the ship by noon for data input and a NISA-ordered siesta. When John failed to show, they had hailed him on his radio but received no response. With mounting anxiety, they had set out, following his rover tracks.

"Good grief!" Joe said, walking over to the other two. "Here's your monster bear. It must have been the last picture John took before he ran away." Dave and Dean could hardly believe what they saw. From looking at the bushes in front of them, they could estimate just how massive the strange-looking bear had been.

Dean covered his face with his hand, then said, "We'd better get on his trail and see what happened."

Climbing back into their individual rovers, everyone was quiet as they drove along. They were each hoping for the best. After all, John did have a taser.

"Hey," Dave told his friends, "I knew that picture kinda reminded me of something. And, I just figured out what it was. One time, when I was about 14, our class went to a real nice museum downtown. It had an Ice Age exhibit. They had several large bear-like creatures in the display. They were called short-faced bears."

Dean pulled his rover to a stop. "Yeah, I've studied those. They were said to be 50% bigger than the largest of our modern bears." Then, his face went pale, and he quickly put his rover back in gear. And, with growing fear, they all sped along John's running prints as fast as their rovers would go.

Joe rounded a group of bushes, then pulled to a quick stop. "Look, you guys!" he shouted with relief in his voice. "Here's where John's rover must have been parked."

Dave pulled up and looked at a set of rover tracks heading to the north. "At least we know that he made it to his rover."

"Yeah," Dean agreed, "but, we also know that those giant bear things were right behind him. Let's get moving."

Up on the ice sheet, the three men easily followed John's rover tracks around the large hills of glacier-deposited dirt and rubble. Joe was once again in the lead. As he started to steer around a pair of large boulders, he suddenly gave a loud shout and spun his wheels to the right.

Dave and Dean watched in horror as a giant beast came charging out from behind the boulders chasing after Joe's rover. The animal was easily 5 feet at the shoulders and at least 11 feet long. It was covered in thick brown fur and had two large horns coming out of the face on its massive head.

"I can't believe it!" Dean shouted to Dave. "It's a…it's a woolly rhinoceros!"

"Whatever it is," Dave shouted back, "it's gaining on Joe!"

"You go that way!" Dean directed. "I'll charge it from this side. Use your horn and shout. Maybe we can get it to back off."

Dave had thought it was a joke that NISA had included horns on their rovers. I mean, who needs a horn on a probably non-existent planet, right? And, even if it did exist, who would there be to honk at? But now, he laid on his horn with everything he had and shouted with all his might.

The rhino stopped chasing Joe right away. First, it charged Dean's rover. Then, it spun around to charge Dave's. And, once Joe joined in the fight, the beast turned with its tail held high and used its speed to get away from all the noise and confusion.

"And don't come back ya big bully!" Dave yelled at the retreating rhino.

"This is, like, totally bizarre!" Joe said shaking his head. "That was a *Coelodonta* if I've ever seen one—which I haven't, since they died out on Earth about 40,000 years ago."

"Let's get going," Dean said. "Now we know it's not just giant bears John has to worry about."

****

When the terrain got too rough, John parked his rover in a sunny spot (to allow its solar-powered batteries to recharge) and started climbing a small icy mountain to try and figure out where he was.

It just wasn't making any sense. Where was he? And, why was he wherever he was? The only thing John seemed to know for certain was that his name was John and that he was (or had been) driving a small, solar-powered rover over what appeared to be the tail of a glacier. Oh, and he also knew that he was lost. Yep, that part was painfully clear. Reaching up to rub his head, he guessed it was that large lump that was keeping him from knowing the answers to his growing list of questions.

From his vantage point, John could see pretty well around him. Here and there in the distance he could see the shapes of a few large animals. Some of them in pairs, but mostly solo. He wondered what they were. Sitting down on a rock, he felt despair settle into his gut. Was he all alone? Was he left behind? Was there anyone who would be looking for him? John felt very afraid.

Strangely, he found himself looking up to the sky. "I need Your help," he said out loud. "Oh Lord, come quickly to help me." After pausing for a moment, John smiled to himself. Well, he hadn't forgotten everything. He knew that, no matter what, there was Someone looking out for him.

John slipped his way back down the little icy mountain and began to explore the contents of his rover. Discovering his turkey and noodles, he bowed his head and gave thanks. It seemed like a sign from heaven that God would indeed take care of him.

After eating, John held up a gun he had found under his seat. It was big for a handgun, but pretty light-weight. He couldn't find any extra ammunition for it. It didn't even seem to have a place to load it anyway.

Suddenly, instinctively, John looked up. About 20 feet up the small mountain, a huge cat-like creature was crouched, getting ready to attack. Where had it come from? John hadn't heard a thing. Hopping out of the rover, John backed away, putting more distance between them. "Go away!" he shouted. "I have a gun."

The cat snarled at the sound of his voice, showing John its giant, six-inch fangs.

"Wow," John said out loud, "I guess your guns look more impressive than mine. But, I'm warning you…mine can reach you from a distance. Yours only work at close range."

As if acknowledging the truth in John's comment, the *Smilodon* began descending the icy rocks.

John tried to keep the rover between him and the 400 pounds of compact muscle that was intent on making him its next meal. As the creature started around the rover, John felt the 'calm before the storm' settle over his body. Everything slowed down. He was ready. But the cat would have to make the first move.

With a snarl, the great cat bounded forward. John waited until he could 'see the whites of its eyes,' then pulled the trigger of his pistol. There was no sound, but the *Smilodon* screamed and stopped advancing. Lowering its head, it re-evaluated its prey. John didn't move, but his brain was flying. This was one weird gun. Nothing had come out of it, but the cat seemed to think something had.

Crouching low, the brute flashed its fangs at John, then took two steps forward. John aimed his weapon and pulled the trigger. The cat screamed again, but this time sprang forward instead of back, knocking John to the ground. It all seemed unreal, like watching a movie. John knew he was about to die.

But, then, instead of sinking its fangs into him, the saber-toothed cat shrieked in pain and spun as if to face some unseen foe. John quickly rolled face down and maneuvered himself under the rover.

"Ha! Ugly Cat!" a voice shouted. "That's the second time you've felt the point of my spear. Do you want to feel it a third time?"

The *Smilodon* growled and spit, but decided it did not want there to be a third time. Turning quickly, it bounded back up the icy mountain.

With relief verging on tears, John pulled himself out from beneath the rover. Getting himself to his feet, he turned to thank his rescuer, who, at that very moment, was coming around the rover to meet him. At that instant, they found themselves face to face. For a moment, both stood stock-still. Then, both men jumped back, opened their mouths and screamed. John raised his taser gun, and Jah-hon raised his spear. They each took two paces back and stared each other down.

John found himself looking at some sort of prehistoric caveman. He was fairly short, but very muscular. His head seemed too big for his body and was topped with a mass of sandy curls. The man-thing's face was broad, with a large forehead that jutted out over hazel eyes. He wore primitive clothes that seemed to be made from animal skins—they were not, however, the kind of clothes you would typically see in pictures of cavemen. He wore warm pants and a warm, long-sleeved top. He also had boots made of fur tied around his feet.

Cautiously, John lowered his taser. He said very slowly, in a loud voice, "Thank you for helping me."

Jah-hon lowered his spear and took a few steps forward. "You're welcome," he answered. Then he added with a note of genuine concern, "What happened to your face? How did it get burned so black?"

John reached up to touch his own face but didn't answer Jah-hon's question. Instead, he said in obvious disbelief, "You can talk…"

Again, they both took a minute to look each other over.

"What kind of animal did you kill to make that coat?" Jah-hon finally asked.

John looked down at his shiny green jacket. "I didn't make it," he answered, "I bought it."

"Oh," Jah-hon said. He had heard about people 'buying' things from his father. "From where do your people come that you are so tall and your skin is so dark brown?"

"I guess from Africa," John answered.

"Where's that?" Jah-hon wondered.

John looked around him in all directions. "I really don't know." He shrugged his shoulders and smiled.

"Where does your family stay?" Jah-hon asked.

"I don't know." John shrugged again. "I hit my head, and I can't seem to remember much of anything…But, I do know my name…I'm John."

"Jah-hon?" Jah-hon repeated with a surprised look on his face.

"Yeah," John said. "John."

"That's *my* name, too…Jah-hon."

"Well, yeah." John smiled. "It's just about the most popular name in the world, ya know."

"It means *God's Gracious Gift*," Jah-hon said. "Did you know that?"

"Yes!" John nodded, then added sincerely. "And, I guess you're God's gift to me, because there is no way I would have survived out here if you hadn't found me."

Jah-hon smiled, then said, "We must hurry back to my cave. My brothers are waiting for me. It will take almost 30 minutes, even if we hurry."

"We can go in the rover," John offered. "It'll be faster."

Jah-hon looked at the rover in surprise. "You mean it's alive?" he asked, taking a step away from it.

"No, it's not alive, but it kind of acts like it is." John smiled. "It's kind of hard to explain. But, I promise it won't hurt you. The only way you can get hurt is if you fall out of it while it's moving."

"So, it's like a sled, only there's nothing pulling it?" Jah-hon said.

"You got it!" John laughed. "Now, you sit here and hold on tight. Show me which way to go, and we'll be back to your cave in no time."

CHAPTER 4

"Okay, now, Darin, you'd better dive on out there and find out if the ship knows when this storm is gonna end," Billy said leaning back against the cave wall.

Darin stood up without a complaint, but turned to David and said, "Remember, *not a word* of the story until I get back." Then, he pulled up his hood and ducked out of the cave.

"So," Dr. Chen rubbed his chin thoughtfully, "would I be accurate in saying that you purposely chose to compare a tall black man to the short Neanderthal-like man—going so far as to give them the same name—with a specific 'point-making' intention?"

"You would be," Billy nodded.

"Would the point you were intending to make," Dr. Chen continued, "be that two people can be physically very different and still be fully human—possessing the ability for a complex language and sophisticated thought-processes?"

"Very perceptive of you, doctor," Billy smiled. "You see," he explained, "most modern anthropologists acknowledge that Neanderthals were indeed human—*Homo sapiens*, like us. However, most still put Neanderthals in a different 'subgroup' from modern man, saying that they didn't belong to the same subgroup modern man 'evolved' from."

"Well," Dr. Chen sat forward, "if anthropologists consider that Neanderthals were *Homo sapiens*, why do creation scientists feel the need to put them in the same 'subgroup' with modern man?"

Billy answered, "I guess it all comes down to one little word...*belief*."

"What about *belief*?" Mark Chen wanted to know.

Taking in a deep breath, then letting it out slowly, Billy explained, "You see, evolutionists *believe* that the world 'created' itself over millions and billions of years. Because of this belief, they take all the real-life evidence they find (such as Neanderthal bones) and try and make it logically fit into their million-year timeline.

"However, creationists *believe* that God created everything in six literal days. Therefore, we take all the real-life evidence (such as Neanderthal bones) and try to show that this evidence can and does fit into the Bible's 6,000 year timeline."

"So," Dr. Chen summarized, "it's because the Bible says God created two specific 'modern-man' people (Adam and Eve) as the 'parents' of all people, that creation scientists want to show that all people have *always* been 'modern-man.' By doing that, you'll be showing that what the Bible says really is true—not just some sort of moral teaching story."

"That's right," Billy answered. "Now, I know quite a few sincere Christian folks who have decided not to takes sides. Instead, they've decided to believe that God created the world *through* evolution. In the short run, this seems to reconcile the 'science' and 'religion' sides of the debate. However, in the long run, there are issues that *will not* fit into this compromise.

"Like what?" Sarah questioned.

David answered, "Well, there's the issue of Adam and Eve. If God created them as the first man and woman, who or what were all the 'sub-humans' some say led up to the first modern man? Were they animals? Did they have souls? Can we really say that the sub-humans that gave birth to Adam and Eve weren't fully human?"

"Or, there's the issue of death," Aaron said. "The Bible says that death didn't enter the world until Adam and Eve sinned. But evolution requires hundreds of millions of years of death just to lead up to Adam and Eve."

"Really," Tasha spoke up, "it's a much bigger issue than most people realize. By accepting evolution's millions of years, people have to reject many of the Bible's foundational truths.

Dr. Chen nodded but was kept from responding by Darin's re-entering the cave and saying excitedly, "The ship said that the coastguard said it should be over in an hour. So you'd better hurry up and finish your story."

"An hour!" Mark gasped. "I'm starved. It's already past lunchtime. I can feel it in my stomach—my very *empty* stomach.

"Well," Billy stood up, "I'll go ahead and hike down to the rafts and get our lunches."

"No!" Mark and Darin both said together. And, reaching up to grab hold of Billy, they both pulled him back down.

"Really," Mark said, "I'm not that hungry. I can wait."

"Yeah," Darin said. "He can wait. Finish the story!"

Dr. Chen laughed. "I have a feeling this story is going to last a while. How about we hear another part, then a couple of us will go get our lunches and give Billy's voice a break."

****

Dusk was settling over the land, and the air was quickly getting colder. As he continued to drive along, Dave reached to pull up the hood of his coat, then called to Dean, "Hey, Chief, once it's dark, maybe John will send up a flare."

Dean shook his head. "I don't see how we could get to him if he did. NISA gave us tops and heaters for our rovers, but nothing that would protect us from a woolly rhino or a short-faced bear. Who knows what will be lurking about after dark?"

"Well, we can't just leave him to freeze to death if we know he's still alive," Dave insisted with a note of anger in his voice.

"Listen, man," Joe turned to Dave as the three rovers pulled up to the ship, "NISA has given him everything he needs to survive temperatures down to 40 below. If John's still alive, the cold is the least of his problems."

As the crew re-entered the ship, Laika greeted them excitedly but then whined nervously at the ship's shut door. She couldn't understand why John wasn't with them. All three of the men were exhausted. After eating a late dinner, they made necessary data entries and then lay down on their bunks in the Zoo.

But, when Laika started to whine by the door again, Dave sat up. "This is crazy! I was told there was less than a 1% chance that this planet would even have the simplest forms of life on it."

Joe sat up, too. "I know what you mean. I thought the start of life on Earth was like a one in a bazillion chance. Who would have expected evolution to be progressing here on T-3 just like it did on Earth?

"Well," Dean said from his bunk, "if God could start life on Earth, why couldn't He start life here on T-3?"

"Who says God had anything to do with any of this—on Earth or on T-3?" Dave asked, flopping back on his bunk.

Joe sighed. "You guys, it doesn't matter if you believe God started the evolutionary process or not. What matters right now is, that from what we can see, T-3 seems to be mirroring Earth's evolutionary progress."

"How can you say God doesn't matter?" Dean challenged Joe. "God is the Giver of life."

"Yeah, yeah!" Dave responded. "That's what *you* think. You sound just like John. But, I say, if God started all this, then He sure isn't taking very good care of His handiwork—at least not back on Earth."

"Come on, you two," Joe interrupted. "We can't jump off into religion right now. We have to stick to science." Turning to Dean, he asked, "So, Chief, you were saying that the animals we've seen match the animals found during Earth's last Ice Age."

"Yeah. And from the little we've seen, I'd put T-3 anywhere from 100,000 to 500,000 years behind Earth."

"So, do you think there are any...you know...uh, people around," Dave asked.

"No modern people," Dean shook his head. "Maybe some close ancestors, like the Neanderthals or some other sub-human creatures—but nobody we could really communicate with."

****

Up at the entrance of the ice cave, John looked up at the stars dimly peeking through the haze. He pulled the thick animal's skin closer around Tah-hommy who had fallen asleep on his lap. It had only taken Jah-hon and John about ten minutes to reach the cave. Jah-hon had said that it was like flying. Once they had parked the rover in the sun, they had climbed up to the cave. Jah-him and Tah-hommy had taken one look at John's tall figure and dark face and had run to the back of the cave. But, after hearing him talk and seeing him eat, they had accepted him. For nearly half an hour after that, Tah-hommy had stood behind John and played with his springy, tight-curled hair.

Then, John had eagerly helped the boys with their afternoon and evening chores. “You’re stronger than you look,” had been Jah-him’s surprising comment.

John had blushed. Something inside of him seemed to know that it was ridiculous that, at 6’1” and 210 pounds, he would be having trouble keeping up with a couple of shrimpy kids. They sure had a lot of power packed into their short bodies.

At dinner, Jah-hon had cooked a ten-pound slab of what he called *sheeka* meat. They had eaten the entire thing. “Well,” John had said, “it’s not Biggie Burgers, but it sure is satisfying.”

“What’s *Biggie Burgers*?” Jah-hon had asked.

“Well,” John had answered with a puzzled look on his face, “I can’t quite remember. But, I’m guessing they never served anyone sheeka meat!”

Now, as the moon rose, and Tah-hommy snored softly on his lap, John’s mind turned back to the one thing he was sure of—God. “Lord,” he prayed quietly, “I feel afraid because I don’t even know who I am, or where I am. But, I thank You that You brought me to this safe place among friends.”

Tah-hommy stirred and looked up at John “My dad prays like that at night. But, my mom usually prays in the morning. She says she’s too tired at night.” Then, he snuggled closer and went back to sleep.

****

It was close to midnight when John woke up to the sound of a deep, low growl. Sitting up on his fur-skin mattress, he looked around. Both Jah-hon and Jah-him were still asleep. Maybe it had just been a dream. He hoped so. Lying back down, he closed his eyes. But, then, there it was again, “Grrrrrroowwllllll…”

****

"Ah, don't worry, John," Tasha broke into the story, "that ain't nothin' but Aaron's stomach growling."

Everyone laughed, and Billy stood up, "Hey, Aaron, why don't you give me a hand getting the lunches."

As the two set off into the rain, Sarah turned to her father. "Daddy, how does Mr. James know that poor Mr. Dean—who died back in the cave—was an astronaut?"

Mark laughed. "Aw, Sarah, Mr. James is just making up a story…"

Sarah shook her head. "No, he said that Dean was married to Susi—just like it said on the poor man's wedding ring."

Dr. Chen came over and ruffled his daughter's hair. "Sweetie, Mr. James just took the names *Dean* and *Susi* to make the story more interesting. He's not trying to tell the *real* story of the man who died back there."

"How do you know?" Sarah pouted. "Everything in his story seems real. You said yourself, that the animals and plants and stuff really used to live around here."

"Well, Mr. James is trying to tell a story that really *could* be true. But, he's just sort of making up all the things that are happening. Do you understand?"

"I guess, kinda," Sarah admitted. "But, I think it's more fun just to believe it really is real."

"So do I!" Tasha said firmly.

CHAPTER 5

When Billy and Aaron returned with the lunches, everyone dug in. Then, Mark brought up an interesting question. "Mr. Billy, did Adam and Eve look like cavemen—like Jah-hon and Tah-hommy?"

Billy wiped his mouth with a napkin, then answered, "I don't know, Mark. But, I doubt it. We really can't be sure *what* Adam and Eve looked like. The only thing we can be sure of is that God made them—the first two people—with enough genetic information between them to produce every different kind of person we see today, and also what we would have seen in the past."

"So," Dr. Chen clarified, "you're saying, what?—that Neanderthals were just one of many people groups that descended from Adam and Eve?"

"Yep." Billy nodded between bites. "You know, look at all of us sitting here. There's black, white, Hispanic, and Asian—not to mention Darin, here, who belongs in his own class."

"Hey!" Darin paused from his task of showing Sarah the intricate art of nibbling out eyes, nose, and a mouth on a slice of bologna.

Billy just smiled, then continued. "Black, white, Hispanic, Asian—we're all one blood—one family—modern humans. It's just that at some point our ancestors were separated and isolated from each other. And the genetic information among those isolated groups changed over time."

"How do you know?" asked Mark.

"There are scientifically documented mutations that we know gave rise to different traits among those isolated groups," Billy answered, "like the various skin and eye colors we see sitting together right here today."

"So, we're all related," Sarah pondered, "even though we look different now."

"All the different people groups trace back to Adam and Eve," Billy reassured her, "and it reveals a wonderfully creative God."

"I must emphatically agree that all the people groups on the earth today are descended from a common, *fully human* ancestor," Dr. Chen said in an almost vehement tone.

The group stopped eating and looked at him. "What's wrong, Daddy?" Sarah asked in a quiet voice.

Dr. Chen sighed. "Oh, Honey, it's just that I guess I've experienced enough prejudice and discrimination to get my emotions up on this issue."

"Oh, I see..." Sarah looked confused. "What's that mean?"

"Well, it's like this," her dad explained. "When someone is different than the majority of people around them, people from the majority group tend to look down on the person who is different. They assume that because that person is different, or speaks with an accent, they must be inferior—or, not as good."

Sarah's expression said that she still didn't understand. So, Tasha tried to explain. "Sarah, most of the people in the United States are white. So, some white people think that white people are superior to (or better than) other groups of people, like blacks or Asians.

"That's dumb," Sarah said, wrinkling up her nose.

"Well…really, it's just *ignorant*," Dr. Chen softened his daughter's response.

"But," David jumped in, "that ignorance has led to some of the very worst horrors in history."

Everyone was quiet for a minute, until Sarah prompted, "Like what?"

"Sarah," Dr. Chen began, "remember some of the things Mark talked about studying in history class…black slavery, the Jewish Holocaust, and the suppression of the Australian Aborigines? These horrible events all stemmed from one people group thinking that they were better than another people group."

"And," Billy said to Dr. Chen, "you should know that *evolution* is the driving force behind each of the examples you just gave."

Mark shook his head. "I don't get it. What does evolution have to do with prejudice?"

"Well, consider," Billy said, "how could intelligent, civilized people *ever* think it was okay to enslave or massacre another group of people? Ultimately, it comes down to sin. These people want to rule and abuse another group of people for their own gain. But, what can they choose to '*believe*' that would enable them to excuse what they're doing? What can they believe to make it seem 'okay'? Well, they have to believe that they are genetically superior to that other group of people."

"I still don't see the connection," Mark looked frustrated.

"Son," Dr. Chen said, "people used to say that blacks were not as evolved as whites. They seemed to think that the lighter your skin was, the farther up you were on the evolutionary timeline. So, some whites thought it was okay to own and use blacks like they would 'other animals.'"

Understanding dawned on Mark's face, and he asked in astonishment, "Are you saying that some people used to think that blacks weren't fully human?"

Darin looked pretty solemn when he answered. "Yeah, that's what we're saying. Isn't it awful?"

"Well," Tasha put in, "that can make reasonable sense *if* you believe people evolved from animals."

"Wow!" Sarah said. "You don't really think we evolved from animals, do you, Daddy?"

"Well, Hon," Dr. Chen smiled, "let's see what Billy has to say in the rest of his story."

****

The next morning, John and his new friends ate some sort of thick stew made up of several kinds of plants. John decided he preferred the sheeka meat. Then they all headed down to take a ride in the rover. First, they took all the extra cargo out and stored it safely among some rocks. Then, John had Tah-hommy sit on Jah-him's lap in the now-empty cargo space. And he had Jah-hon sit on the divider between the front and the back of the rover. Of course, his legs and feet had to find whatever space was left on either side of John. Then, after making sure everyone had something solid to hold on to, John was off—taking the young 'cavemen' on the joy ride of their lives.

After an hour of exploration, however, a red light at the front of the rover began to blink and beep. John read it out loud to the others. "Low fuel—recharge battery."

"That's easy," John assured them. "See the arrow pointing down? I just push this button…" As John pushed the button, several solar panels automatically adjusted to absorb the sun's powerful rays.

"My grandfather could read," Jah-hon commented. "And Dad said there are people who live off the ice that can read."

"Why doesn't your family live off the ice?" John asked as they climbed out of the rover and headed away from the ice sheet and toward a small lake Jah-hon said was full of fish.

Jah-him shrugged. "Dad likes it right near the edge. He says, that way, we can have the best of both worlds."

John made a face. "What's good about freezing cold snow and ice?"

"It keeps our food from spoiling," Jah-hon pointed out practically. "And, there's a lot fewer bugs and pesky little critters on the ice."

"And," Jah-him added, "a lot fewer giant beasts to get mad at us on the ice."

"And," Tah-hommy said with wide eyes, "a lot fewer *dragons* to eat us."

"Dragons?" John said in disbelief. "Come on, Tommy, you're old enough to know dragons aren't real."

Jah-hon, Jah-him, and Tah-hommy all stopped and stared at John like he was crazy. "Everyone knows dragons are real," Jah-him stated with confidence. "I've even seen some of the smaller ones. But, two years ago, Dad saw one that was 40 feet long and over 15 feet tall."

"No way!" John was shocked. "Where did he see it?"

"He was a four day's walk south of the ice," Jah-hon explained. "Seeing such a big one was one of the reasons he decided to stay on the ice."

"Why don't the, uh, dragons come close to the ice?" John asked, glancing nervously around at the shoulder high bushes and small trees growing up out of the icy mud.

"Too cold," Jah-him answered. "Anyway, our grandpa used to tell us the stories his grandpa told him. His grandpa was Papa Jah-eff-ahth. Papa Jah-eff-ahth lived even before the Great Disaster. He said there used to be great herds of all kinds of dragons. Whole areas of the world were dominated by dragons. Grandpa also told us that most dragons used to be about like the deer we sometimes see—they ate plants, and didn't bother you, unless you made them angry."

"Hmmm," John said, "I always thought dragons were fierce loners that could fly and breathe fire."

"Dad says that there are stories of dragons that could breathe fire," Jah-hon said. "I've never seen that, but we know that some dragons can fly. We see them at the end of each summer, just before it turns cold."

"When I was 12," Jah-him said excitedly, "we saw a whole flock of sharp-tails. They are twice as big as the brown-wings we usually see."

Tah-hommy got excited too, pulling his hand out of Jah-him's, he shouted, "I want to see a spear-head. Daddy says its head is as big as I am! And, he said he saw one once flying up over Green Lake. Maybe there will be one over our fishing lake…" and he started to run ahead to the water that was now in sight.

But Jah-hon caught him by the arm and gave his shoulder a little shake. "Tah-hommy, you know the rules! We have to stay together. You never know what might be waiting to eat you for lunch."

Tah-hommy looked sorry and a little scared. He turned to John. "Can I ride on your back? You're so tall, nothing will be able to eat me for lunch."

John took out his taser and set it for the strongest stun, then he let Tah-hommy climb on his back.

****

Dean, Joe, and Dave had their rovers grouped together in a sort of three-pointed star, with their headlights pointed outward. Laika sat alert in Joe's rover. The men had been up at the crack of dawn to continue their search for John.

Now, they had stopped for lunch and a brief rest. It had been on a whim that Joe had decided to bring Laika along. But, she had turned out to be as indispensable here as tornado sirens are in Kansas. Already, five times that morning, her barks had alerted them to curious animals of immense size.

The worst had been a pair of giant hyena-like creatures. Dean had called them *Megistotheriums*. Whatever they were, they had been hungry enough to attack. It had taken five sharp stuns to make them change their minds. But, the strangest of the creatures they had seen was the *Megatherium*, or giant ground sloth. It was so big, it seemed unreal—as big as an elephant. But, it had been easily outrun, which was a very good thing, since no amount of stuns would have done any good.

"I give up on NISA regulations," Dave said as soon as he finished his lunch. He climbed out of his rover, walked over to a very small tree, and cut it down with his knife. Then, he broke out six feet of the strong middle section. Stripping off its little branches, he took some string and strapped his biggest knife securely to one end of the stick. "NISA's on the other side of the sun. They didn't even expect there to be multi-cellular life on T-3. I'm sure all those chair-bound computer geeks would be the first to change their *no-kill* rules if they were the ones facing prehistoric monsters."

Neither Dean nor Joe said a word to contradict him. Instead, they both got out of their rovers and found their own suitable saplings to turn into long-handled spears.

After completing their new weapons, the three continued to drive along in search of clues to where John might have gone. "Well, at least we know why he's not answering our calls," Joe said looking down at John's recovered communicator.

"I think it's definitely a good sign," Dean answered. "Only the band of the communicator was broken, and there were no signs of blood or violence."

Laika gave three quick, sharp barks, and the Discovery's crew braked their rovers to look at a herd of eight medium-sized deer-like animals that had turned toward them in response to Laika's bark.

"Man," Joe said as he snapped a few pictures, "those are the smallest things we've seen on this trip, besides insects and birds."

"There are smaller animals," Dean responded. "I've seen their tracks. I guess they just skedaddle before we get a chance to see them."

"At least we don't have to worry about any dinosaurs," Joe laughed. "According to Earth's timeline, they should have died out millions of years ago."

Dean smiled on the outside, but on the inside his mind was racing. Where could John have gone? Why hadn't he tried to contact them? As the captain of the Discovery's crew, John was *his* responsibility. Why didn't he have any answers?

Then, although there didn't seem to be any reason for it, the deer suddenly spooked and turned to bound off. Laika sniffed the air and began to whimper. Dave put down his camera and began to move his rover ahead. "Whatever spooked the deer is spooking Laika. Let's get out of here." Dean and Joe put their rovers in gear, glancing at the bushes around them as they moved forward.

Suddenly, a group of four green animals with brown markings came out from behind a large deposit of rocks and dirt and blocked their way. Joe, who was in the lead, turned north—speeding up. The other rovers followed his lead. But, to their dismay, they found that three other similar creatures had been coming up behind them. Now, all seven rose up tall on their big hind legs, and the chase was on.

Dean quickly surmised that these were not mammals. Whatever they were, they had very little trouble keeping up with the rovers on the rough terrain. They didn't seem ready to attack. It seemed more like they were trying to figure out what the men, and dog, and rovers were, and how they were or were not connected to each other. Bottom line—were these unknown animals something good to eat?

They had large heads, skinny arms, huge mouths full of sharp teeth, and were approximately twelve feet long and five feet tall with a long stiff tail. Dave gulped as he saw the flash of one large sharp claw on each of the creatures' hind feet. Deinonychus!

The chase lasted fifteen minutes. As soon as the ground under them got too cold, the reptilian pack gave up its chase and turned back south.

Slowing their rovers to a stop, all three men pushed their *recharge* buttons. They wouldn't want to run out of power in the middle of any future chases.

"So, Dave!" Dean called. "What happened to *no dinosaurs*?"

"I don't know..." Dave pondered. "Maybe T-3 never got hit by a big asteroid like Earth did. If there was no asteroid, I guess there wouldn't have been all the damage that brought about the onset of an ice age...so, maybe, there wasn't a major dinosaur die-out here."

"From the looks of things when we surveyed the planet before landing, there's an ice age going on right now," Joe commented with a smirk. "Why would there be *this* ice age, if there wasn't an asteroid?"

"I guess T-3 could have just had its asteroid recently, a long time after Earth had hers," Dave guessed.

"But," Dean disagreed, "it's supposed to be because of the asteroid millions of years ago that the mammals got ahead of the reptiles on Earth. So, why do we see all these large mammals here if this is just the *first* ice age?"

"Don't ask me!" Dave snapped. "I just want to find John and get out of here!"

Joe and Dean both nodded. But they all knew that if they had had this much trouble as a group, John's chances of surviving alone were getting pretty slim.

****

"Hey, Doc," Billy turned to Dr. Chen. "Looks like the rain's back to a drizzle. What do you say we head on out to the gull colony Darin had spotted? Maybe we can get that one done before we have to head back to the ship."

Nobody moved, not even Dr. Chen. "Well…" he said, "I guess that *is* why we're here…"

"Yep," Billy said standing up. "Don't worry, y'all, I'll finish the story back on the *Scandinavian*."

Still, no one moved. Mark, Sarah, *and* Darin were all giving Dr. Chen their most beguiling, pleading expressions.

"Well…" Dr. Chen started again, "I'm guessing all that hard rain kept the gulls from feeding. If we go near their nests, we'll just be keeping them on the ground longer. So… *scientifically*, it would be best if we don't disturb the birds for a while."

Everyone cheered. Then, Mark and David hopped up to once again pull Billy back down to the cave floor.

As soon as Billy got comfortable, Dr. Chen was ready with a question. "It seems that your story is saying that it was *not* an asteroid that wiped out the dinosaurs and brought on the first ice age. If not that, then what caused the earth to change from a warm, moist paradise, to a mostly frozen no-man's land?"

"First of all," Billy said, "to set the record straight, creationists follow the biblical timeline of 6,000 years. Therefore, we don't believe in 'several' long ice-ages. Instead, we believe that the scientific evidence fits the model of one Ice Age—which included many shorter periods of terrible blizzards—with the whole Ice Age lasting maybe 500 years."

"Okay…" Dr. Chen took that in. "You can explain that in greater detail later. For now, what do you think caused the earth to change from a paradise to a snowball?"

"I hinted at that in the story already…" Billy smiled.

"I know! I know!" Darin raised his hand.

"That's cheating," David said, pulling Darin's hand down. "Of course *you* know the answer."

Tasha smiled. "Go on, Billy, tell the rest of the story. Then, Dr. Chen can figure it out on his own."

CHAPTER 6

The fishing had been very successful, with Jah-hon spearing more than 20 fish. Jah-him had caught ten, and even John had gotten three. Jah-hon and Jah-him had taken turns cleaning the fish the others caught. They threw the heads, tails, scales, and insides quickly back into the lake.

But, then, as they got ready to head out, John was surprised to see Jah-hon leave five of the biggest fish scattered by the shore. Still, he thought, they had almost more than they could carry back to the rover. However, when Jah-him dropped three of his own along the way, John couldn't keep quiet. "Hey, Jim! Man, whatcha doin'? If you can't handle your load, I'll carry some for you."

"Don't worry," Jah-hon smiled. "We catch the ugly fish on purpose. They're big, but they taste nasty."

"Okay, I think I'll need this one explained," John sighed.

"Dad taught us to always leave an offering behind—no matter what we kill," Jah-him said solemnly.

"Why?" John looked surprised. "Is it some sort of religious ritual?"

Jah-him and Tah-hommy were shocked at John's question and looked uncomfortably at the ground. Jah-hon asked in a cautious tone, "We thought you believed in the one true God who made all that there is. How can you talk about religious rituals like the people of the west who have forsaken the true God for made-up false gods?"

"Whoa!" John said as they began to load the fish into the bottom of the rover. "I do believe in the true God. I'm just wondering why you would leave fish as an offering."

Jah-hon visibly relaxed. "We're not leaving the fish as an offering to a god! Where are you from, anyway, that you know how to read and drive this strange rover, but you don't know the first thing about safety?"

"I wish I knew," John sighed as he watched Tah-hommy lay three more of their fish on the ground before they drove off.

"It's like this," Jah-hon explained from his perch on the rover's divider. "Whenever we make a kill, there are always noses that smell our catch. Those noses are attached to very large, dangerous creatures that are almost always hungry. Now, if we leave parts of our kill behind, the bears and hyenas…"

"And, *dragons*," Tah-hommy added in.

"And, dragons," Jah-hon agreed, "will take the time to stop and eat what we've left. By that time, we'll be quite a bit ahead of them. And, when we get on the ice, most of the animals don't bother following."

"Makes sense to me," John said as the rover pulled its way up onto the slushy melting snow of the edge of the glacier. "But, don't the animals just follow your smell—thinking they'll find more food."

"You've got your brain moving now!" Jah-hon laughed. "That is a possibility, but most animals won't follow us onto the ice." After a pause, Jah-hon continued, "It's the people who live off the ice that have to worry the most. They have to build cities with walls, and post guards. I can't imagine living like they do."

"But," John contended, "it's warm, you could have friends to spend time with, all the food you needed right close by…"

"Yeah," Jah-hon said with a frown. "It *sounds* good. But it just leads to trouble. When all those people get together, just like they did after the Great Disaster, everything starts going downhill. The people soon reject God's good rules and…they start doing all the horrible things the people from the west do."

John smiled to himself as he drove a wide arc around yet another big, hairy elephant. Even after only a day, he knew that if you didn't bother them, they wouldn't bother you. He did wonder where they found enough food to satisfy their big stomachs.

"All the elephants I've ever seen are bald, with shorter tusks," John remarked. "I'll bet Dean would love to see one of these hairy guys."

"Who's Dean?" Jah-hon asked in surprise.

"Well…um, I'm not sure. I guess he must be someone I know who likes elephants," John said, rubbing what remained of the bump on his head.

Jah-hon gave John a slap on the shoulder. "Seems like maybe you're starting to remember some things."

"I hope so," John answered with new optimism. "I wonder where I come from? I hope that I don't belong to the strange people from the west you're always talking about."

"Who knows? Maybe you do," Jah-hon smiled. "Mom says that God keeps His remnant, even in the worst places." But, then he added, "I'd guess you're from the far south. Dad has relatives in the south. He said that some of his uncles have darker skin—but, I didn't think he meant as dark as yours. Maybe just a little darker than Wah-ulf and Suh-mer."

"Where are they from?" John asked as they neared the base of the hill that held the home cave.

"From the far east," Jah-hon said. "They lived up north with Mom's people until they learned our language. A few years ago, they traveled down with Mom's uncle's family and decided to stay with us on the edge of the ice."

"Why?" John wondered.

"It's because Jah-honny, here, is so good lookin'!" Jah-him laughed and then made some kissy sounds. "They think he'll make a good man for one of their girls."

Jah-hon blushed, but couldn't do anything about Jah-him's teasing, since he was filling his arms with fish to carry up to the cave.

"Wah-ulf has three daughters and no sons," Jah-hon said. "I guess he used to have two sons as well, but one was killed in one of those awful cities. That's why they left the east. Then, the oldest son died when the ice unexpectedly opened up, as it sometimes does farther up north. It can swallow you whole."

John shivered, then asked in a teasing tone, "So, Johnny-boy, you got your eye on any of Wah-ulf's girls in particular?"

Jah-hon blushed again. And Tah-hommy answered for him. "He likes Whin-die. She's nice, and pretty, too."

Jah-hon rolled his eyes. "Tah-him gets first pick, he's the oldest."

John looked closely at Jah-hon. "How old are you?"

Jah-hon tried to stand a little taller as he answered, "I'm 18. Jah-him is 14. And, Little Tah-hommy is 6. Tah-him is 24. We expect him to get married next spring."

Getting the fish up to the cave ended up taking two trips. Jah-him stayed in the cave to build up a fire to cook the fish. "So," John asked, "Does Tim like any of Wah-ulf's girls?"

"Well…" Jah-hon hesitated, "he has given his opinion to Dad…but he will leave the final decision to Wah-ulf and Dad."

"What?" John stopped in mid-step. "Wha-chu-talkin' 'bout, man! Come on! I'd think your brother is old enough and smart enough to pick for himself!"

"He is old enough and smart enough…" Jah-hon answered slowly. "But, you see, that's what happened before the Great Disaster. They stopped trusting the advice of their parents and started marrying whomever they wanted—even those who had rejected the true God. That's how the people of the west live today. And now look at them!"

****

Dave sat outside in his rover, even though Joe and Dean had climbed back up into the ship after another long day of searching for John. Laika was curled up behind him on the rover's cargo box. She was resting, but always alert.

As Dave watched the sun slip behind the horizon, he leaned forward. "God," he said in a low, earnest tone, "John's always saying You're everywhere. So, I guess You're here on T-3, too. Anyway, God, You know, John's been my best friend. I mean, he's a good man. And, You know, he's one of Your people…" The sun was gone, and a few birds fluttered in the bushes nearby, but Dave didn't notice. "I guess, God, I've tried really hard not to believe in You…I guess that was dumb. Anyway, please…will You please help us find John…I mean, find him alive and okay…please…"

Laika sat up and a low growl started in her throat. Dave had her tucked under his arm and was heading up to the ship's entry before she even had a chance to bark. He wasn't about to wait around and see what might be lurking in the darkness.

****

"It's…well, it's the tradition of our people. Always has been," Jah-him tried to explain to John as they all headed down to the rover early the next morning.

"So," John turned to Jah-hon, "you're saying that if you can see a star during the day, then it's a sign that God is going to send you some kind of special help?"

"That's what we've been told," Jah-hon nodded.

"And," John questioned, "you said that a few days before you found me, you two saw a star during the day?"

"Yes, yes!" Jah-him answered excitedly. "It was big and bright and shining. And it seemed to be falling out of the sky. But, then it disappeared behind a hill, and we couldn't see it anymore."

"Why don't we go and look for it?" John said as any true explorer would.

Jah-hon shook his head. "How can you find the *Lord's star*? Anyway, this morning it is our family's turn to check the *Vast West Wall*."

Climbing into the rover, Jah-hon smiled. "It used to take Dad and Tah-him and me from sunup to sundown to do this. But, with your rover, it won't take much time at all. And this will be the first time Tah-hommy has ever gone so far from home. I wonder why more of your people haven't brought these rovers up here to trade with us. I'll bet Mom's people would trade three years' worth of furs just for one."

John smiled, but didn't say anything. He had woken up that morning feeling extra confused. It wasn't that he couldn't remember anything anymore. It was more like he remembered little bits and pieces of too many things. The result left his mind spinning.

An hour's drive mostly north brought the group up to the foot of an icy mountain. They parked the rover in the sun to recharge, then started the long, upward climb.

Something told John that he'd done this sort of thing before. Stretching his long arms and legs from one little ledge to the next, John was soon quite a bit ahead of the others. Looking down from one of the larger ice ledges, he took in the hugeness of the glacier around him. Its whiteness reached as far north as he could see. It also stretched quite a ways to the west. Large shaggy animals dotted the ice.

John was eager to get to the top to see what lay to the east. So, he carefully climbed back down to the others and had Tah-hommy climb onto his back. Using a leather cord to secure him in place, John took up the rear, and they all followed Jah-hon who knew right where they needed to go.

By the time they'd all reached the top, John had had his first *solid* memory. He could remember climbing a mountain with a heavy weight on his back. Climbing with him had been another man—a white guy with a smirk of a smile. "Dave," John said out loud.

"Who's Dave?" Tah-hommy asked as he climbed off John's back.

"He's my best friend," John answered. "And, he has light skin like you guys, but he's tall and slim like me."

"Did he come north with you?" Jah-hon asked, trying to get John to remember more.

"I'm not sure," John said in a frustrated tone. "It feels like I *almost* know, but I just don't."

Going over a final small hill, Jah-hon pointed to a large, cold-water lake that filled the top of the mountain. There were large deposits of dirt and small, hardy plants that grew up all around. It looked more like a spring thaw than the top of an ice mountain.

"This is Green Lake. It is places like these that feed many of the animals who live on the ice," Jah-hon explained. "Unfortunately, it is not a very stable place. Only outcasts live here—and lots and lots of predators," Jah-hon added, pulling his short-handled spear out of the back of his belt.

"John," Jah-hon motioned to him. "You work with me. Tah-hommy can watch. Jah-him, you go set a few ice traps for hoppers. I hope we can catch a few, otherwise we'll have to have fish again before we head back down."

John followed his younger friend with lots of questions. "What's a hopper? And, what's that stick for? Why do you have those lines on your arms? How long is this gonna take?"

Jah-hon held up his hand. "I'll explain," he laughed. "When we moved here, we took over the cave of one of Mom's relatives who had decided to move back up north. However, with the cave came a responsibility. Once every seven days during the warm months, someone must check the Vast Wall."

Jah-hon walked out onto a sort of ice-bridge. To the east was the large lake. To the west was the side of the mountain they had just been climbing.

Spreading out his hands, Jah-hon said, "This is the Vast Wall. It divides all the people who live for a hundred miles to the west, and 20 miles to the north, and many hundreds of miles to the south from the immeasurable amount of water trapped here in Green Lake. The four families that live within a couple miles of the Wall take turns measuring and checking its thickness once a week during the warm months."

"If the Vast Wall breaks," Tah-hommy said with round eyes, "we will all die, just like in the Great Disaster."

"So, there's reason to believe that the Wall is getting thinner and weaker?" John asked a bit nervously as he looked out over the huge lake.

"Most years it loses a foot or two more than it gains back the following winter," Jah-hon explained. "But this year, Dad thinks it's reaching a critical point. He says that we might have to move up north with Mom's relatives next spring."

"Why not move east of the lake?" John asked. "It would only be a few miles to the other side."

"Nobody lives for 200 miles to the east." Jah-hon shook his head. "It's not livable—at least not for people. Much of it is slushy swampy ice during the summer and mile after mile of big broken hunks of ice piled up on top of each other during the winter."

Jah-hon had his stick out and was measuring end-to-end along a straight groove that had obviously been purposely cut by someone. And, all along the groove was some sort of orange dye.

"Here," Jah-hon said, handing John a crooked but strong stick. "You follow behind me and make the groove a little bit deeper, so that it will still be here next week."

Then, he handed Tah-hommy a medium-sized bag. "Here's the dye, Tah-hommy. You can follow John and put new color on it. Just don't use too much at once, the powder in the bag has to last you all the way over to the lake." It was as if Jah-hon had just crowned Tah-hommy king of the hill, he was so pleased with his new job.

Once the measuring was done, Jah-hon made some marks in the ice, then on his arm. Then, he shook his head and started to measure all over again.

By this time, Jah-him was back with them. "What's wrong, Jah-honny?" he asked in a serious voice.

"Well," Jah-hon said, "according to the marks Wah-ulf put on my arm, there are supposed to be 20 marks, each a certain amount of sticks apart. But, maybe Wah-ulf made a mistake. I can't believe we've really lost two whole marks in the last week. That's *twice* the amount we usually lose in an *entire summer!"*

Everyone watched tensely as Jah-hon re-measured, and checked the marks on his arms, and checked the colors of the smaller lines that ran perpendicular to the long orange line.

Finally, he took John's stick and dug a deep long groove 10 feet from the lake shore, then another at 20, and another at 30 feet. Taking out a smaller bag of blue powdered dye, he filled the grooves, and the dye spread out into the wet ice.

"Jah-him, go see if you've caught anything in your traps," Jah-hon said. "We've got to get going. We need to leave right away and find Dad."

"Yea!" Tah-hommy clapped his hands excitedly. "We get to go see Daddy!"

John knew it wasn't time for questions. Instead, he told Tah-hommy to get on his back so he could strap him on.

Jah-him came back with two medium-sized animals. John thought they looked a lot like small kangaroos, or maybe wallabies, but fluffier. Jah-him tied one to Jah-hon's back, then Jah-hon tied the other to Jah-him's back. Then, without a word, they headed down the mountain.

About halfway down, Jah-hon paused and looked back over his shoulder. "Something's following us. Probably something after our food, since we didn't leave an offering."

Two-thirds of the way down, Jah-hon's words were proven true as a medium-sized knife-tooth appeared from behind an icy ridge. Snarling, it showed the group its incredibly long canine teeth. In the blink of an eye, Jah-hon had pulled out his spear. But, John put up his hand and pushed the spear tip down, then stepped in front of Jah-hon. Aiming his taser, he sent a strong shock right at the creature's sensitive pink nose. The poor kitty shot straight into the air and did a back flip. Then, once it had regained its footing, it turned tail and bounded out of sight.

John smiled at the others. "I figured we didn't have time for a spear fight."

All the boys laughed and hurried on down toward the rover that would take them off the ice and out to the western fields where their father was hunting with the others.

CHAPTER 7

Dean pulled his rover closer to Joe's as the three drove west in search of their missing crew member. "Uh, Joe...Dave and I have been talking about what happens if we reach the 10-day mark without finding John."

"Man," Joe sighed. "I can't even think about leaving John behind."

"Well," Dean continued, "Dave and I have agreed that if we find enough evidence to make us think that John might still be alive, then, well...one of us will stay behind. That way, if we find each other, we'll have another person to stay with until another ship could come back."

"No way!" Joe slammed on his rover breaks. "No way! You can't stay here on this Ice Age planet with giant beasts and dinosaurs. Chief, if we can't find John, you know that NISA would say we are under orders to prepare a memorial for him, and then return to Earth—all of us."

"Yes, we all know what the New International Space Agency would say," Dean nodded. "But, in the end, we have to do what we can live with. Neither Dave nor I can live with leaving John here alone if there's a chance that he's alive."

At this point, Dave pulled up with them. "Are you crazy?" Joe asked him with a hint of fear in his voice. "You can't just stay here and hope you'll somehow meet up with John. Man, listen, we can leave a bunch of our stuff at the campsite. That way, if he's okay, he can find it and use it."

"No, Joe, you listen," Dave said firmly. "If *you* were lost in the Ice Age, would you rather be alone with a bunch of cool survival surplus or skip the surplus and have a friend?"

The obvious answer made Joe defensive. "Hey, what are you doing, trying to be some kind of a hero or something?"

"Joe," Dean interrupted, "we're not asking *you* to stay. The ship needs your know-how to get back."

"Well," Joe turned to Dean, "what about you? Your wife is back home waiting for you."

"That's why he's not staying—I am," Dave answered for Dean, then drove on ahead of the others.

After the crew had gone nearly three hours to the west, they had to stop to recharge their rovers in the high sun. Laika sniffed around, occasionally chasing the big insects that hopped and flew close to the ground. Then, all of the sudden, her nose went straight to the ground. Looking back at her human companions, she gave two quick barks, then took off. Dave grabbed up his taser and spear and ran to where Laika had been. Bending down, he looked at the ground. Then, jumping up, he started to run after Laika. "Come on you two," he called back. "Laika's found John!"

****

Everyone in the cave stayed quiet and still. But, when Billy stood up, they came to life, all protesting the break in the story. But Billy didn't give in. "My backside needs a walk," he declared. "Besides, look, the rain's done. Let's see how the water on the bay is. If it's calm enough, we can head on back to the *Scandinavian*."

David, Mark, and Aaron exploded out the cave entrance at full speed, but came to a sudden and slippery halt after only a dozen steps. "Ah, man!" Aaron said. "Bad news!"

"What's wrong?" Darin asked, stepping out. Then, he exclaimed, "Crum-hum-biddly-bummer-BUM!" after slipping and falling hard onto his back pockets.

Of course, then everyone walked out to see what was going on. Ice. Everything was coated in a slick layer of ice. "I can't believe this!" Billy said.

"Oh, Daddy," Sarah said, "all our baby birds…Will they be okay?"

Dr. Chen looked pretty sober. "I don't know Sarah. If this cold snap only lasts tonight, I think most of them will survive. But, if it lasts…"

"But, Dad," Mark turned to his father, "what about us? Will we be okay?"

"'Will we be *okay*?'" Billy roared in a cheerful tone. "Don't you worry about a thing, Mark. Just reset your gauge to *adventure mode*. If we have to stay here tonight, it will just be one big adventure."

With this encouragement, all the young people started to laugh and holler and pass around high-fives. Dr. Chen looked a bit worried, but chose to smile for the sake of the kids. Billy sat down in the cave and took off his shoes, then peeled off his socks.

"Whatcha doing, Mr. Billy?" Sarah asked.

Billy smiled. "I'm gonna rub my socks in this here cave dirt, then tie them around my boots so that I have some traction on these icy rocks. I need to get up a little ways to let the ship know that we're gonna need to stay here till morning. No way can we get safely down to our rafts. But, we have all we need in our packs. I'm guessing the morning sun will melt this ice right quick."

As soon as Billy was out of sight, Dr. Chen turned to Darin with a devious smile. "Well now, young man, it is my understanding that you have a weakness for delicious desserts."

Darin turned an interested, but guarded, eye toward Dr. Chen. "Maybe, and maybe not. Why do you ask?"

"Oh, it's nothing much. I just have a few little *issues* in Billy's story I'd like made a bit more…clear."

"No, sir, Doc," Darin shook his head resolutely. "Billy told me specifically not to answer any questions about the story."

"Hey, Sarah," Dr. Chen nodded to his daughter. "Why don't you tell Darin all about your mother's banana-split ice cream cake."

Darin swallowed hard and took two steps back, then covered his ears and began singing, "La la la—I can't hear you—la la la."

Sarah walked toward Darin and said in a louder voice, "Three layers of made-from-scratch white cake…"

Mark joined in. "Fresh strawberries, ripe bananas, and rich hot fudge…"

"Stop! Stop!" Darin cried out. "Okay, how about if I answer one question? Will you give me the recipe?"

Dr. Chen shook his head and held up two fingers.

"Creamy chocolate and vanilla ice cream…" Sarah continued.

Darin looked to David for help. "David-dude, you gotta help me out here."

"Steady, Darin," David encouraged his friend. "You can do it. Just say *no* to temptation."

Aaron shook his head. "He's lost. *Mr. Sweet Treat* ain't got a chance."

Mark stepped forward. "Man, Darin, just picture all that real whipped cream all piled…"

Suddenly, Darin rushed forward, "Okay! Okay! I'll answer two questions in exchange for the recipe."

Dr. Chen smiled. Rubbing his hands together, he said, "Let's see…First, what is the 'Great Disaster' Jah-hon's family keeps referring to? And, second, what *did* cause the climactic changes and eventual Ice Age if it wasn't a meteorite?"

Darin looked discouraged. "Awe, that's just what Billy *doesn't* want you to know. How about something to do with the different animals the crew's met up with?"

"No way!" Dr. Chen frowned. "Now, hurry up and answer if you want that recipe—Billy will be back any second."

"Okay, okay!" Darin said sitting down. "The answer to both your questions is one and the same—*Noah's Flood.* You see, most people just think about rain and water when they think about Noah's Flood. But, in reality, it was a whole lot more than that. It says in the Bible that the heavens were opened, and the springs of the great deep burst forth.

"Scientists have looked closely at the Bible, and it seems to be saying that there could have been giant earthquakes and tsunamis; hundreds, or maybe even thousands of volcanic eruptions; and even billions of gallons of water that had been trapped beneath the earth's crust all bursting forth while the heavens poured down the forty days of torrential rain. All this would have sent more debris than we can imagine into the sky—not just water onto the earth. This debris would have had the same effect evolutionists say was caused by the dust and debris raised up by their meteorite."

"Wow…" Dr. Chen leaned back against the cave wall. "I never, ever heard it explained that way. So, then, why would…"

"No-no, we agreed to two questions, and *Noah's Flood* was the answer to both. Now, you owe me a recipe." With that, Darin raised his hand to his lips and turned an imaginary key, then tucked the 'key' into his pocket for safe keeping.

"Mmm, mmm!" Mark said rubbing his stomach. "Boy, Darin, you should taste my mom's Hot Apple Caramel Melt…"

Darin was just about to try covering his ears and singing again when Billy ducked back into the cave. "The captain of the *Scandinavian* says that a warm front is due to come through here in the next hour. That should melt this ice off lickety-split. He thinks we'll be back on board before they serve up bedtime snack."

"Food, ah—yes," Aaron said rubbing his tummy. "All this talk about supreme desserts has set my stomach to talkin' about fillin' it with some good food!"

"Why were y'all talking about *supreme desserts*?" Billy asked suspiciously.

Mark quickly tried to change the subject by saying in a sad voice, "But, then we'll miss out on our overnight adventure."

"Don't worry, man," David laughed. "It would have been a pretty cold, uncomfortable adventure."

"And," Tasha added, "I'm not so sure I'd like to spend the night with Mr. Bones back there."

"I'm with you!" Sarah said with a shiver.

"So, Billy," Dr. Chen began, "I was wondering, if Noah's Flood caused the Ice Age, why..."

"Hey!" Billy interrupted, then turned suddenly on Darin. "Okay, how much did you tell him?" he asked with his arms folded across his chest.

Darin scooted back a bit and hung his head guiltily. But, Tasha intervened for him. "Don't blame him, Billy. It was beyond his control—*banana-split ice cream cake*. Anyway, I bet he'll share the spoils, won't you Darin?"

Darin nodded so enthusiastically that Billy had to laugh. "Okay, but *I* get the first piece."

Darin smiled and nodded, but whispered aside to David, "Maybe the first, but certainly not the *biggest*..."

CHAPTER 8

Hope and joy grew greater with each human footprint the crew passed as they raced behind Laika's excited barks. But they all drew up short and hesitated when they heard the sound of unintelligible shouts. Laika cried and yipped and came running back to them with rocks falling close behind her.

Dave moved forward cautiously, then crouched down and peeked through the tall grass out into an open area. It was obviously a camp of some sort. All the tall grass had been crushed down into a very large circle. There were four large fire pits with slabs of meat hung high above the flames. Dave gasped and motioned for Dean and Joe to come quietly forward. All three looked on in disbelief at five human-like figures standing protectively around the fires, each with a rock in one hand and a spear in the other.

Whatever they were, they all appeared to be female. After a moment, three of them lowered their weapons and went back to tending the fires. One pulled several slabs of meat off a line and put them on a rock to cool. The youngest of the five stacked already-cooled pieces onto one of two large sleds already piled with layers of dried meat. These sleds were positioned in the very center of the camp, encircled by the fires.

"Incredible," Dave whispered. "These prehistoric creatures are drying and stockpiling meat. Isn't that pretty advanced for this time period?"

As the men took in the details of the camp, Laika began to whimper and tugged at Joe's sleeve. Joe stood up and looked over the grasses around them. He didn't have to look far to see what was upsetting Laika. Two giant hairy beasts were closing in on them. "Dean, Dave!" Joe ducked down to whisper. "Looks like we've got two of those giant bear things heading our way."

Dean stood up and watched the larger of the two bears sway its head back and forth, pausing to sniff the air. "I don't think they're after us," he guessed. "I think it's all that free meat in there that they're after. Let's just move out of their path."

"You're not saying that you're gonna let those bullies go in there and take what they want from a group of helpless girls…?" Joe looked shocked. "Chief, come on, we can't do that!"

"I wouldn't call them *helpless* or *girls*," Dean said as he led the way through the grass a good 200 feet around to the left side of the circular camp.

"Well, we can't just sit here and watch them get mauled," Dave said in a disgusted tone.

"Be quiet," Dean cautioned. "Let's just wait and see what happens. NISA didn't send us here to get killed trying to rescue cavemen—or cave*women*. Besides, how are we supposed to find John if we're all chewed up inside the stomach of a giant bear?"

Dave faced Dean. "Dude, your logic is way off! You can't be saying we let these five people get killed in the name of our *maybe* saving John—only one person. I wouldn't even say that, and John's my best friend!"

Dean's face got red with anger. "These aren't people! Look at them! That short one looks like she's straight off the cover of *Rational Science*. Now, be quiet, the bears are coming closer."

Dave started to say something more, but Dean whispered sternly, "Quiet! That's an order!"

Joe looked confused and didn't seem to know what to think. But Dave shook his head and set his taser on high, grasping his homemade spear a little tighter.

****

Whin-die was the first to see the bears. She called to the others, and walked calmly forward to a pre-prepared pile of stones. Suh-mer called her youngest daughter, Brah-heez, to stand behind her. Soo-sahn, went to stand with the other three to face the bears, while Suh-mer's oldest daughter, Rah-hain, guarded the other side of the camp.

It looked like a mother and an older cub. Everyone waited. They had done this dozens of times over the past week. When the bears were about 50 feet away, Suh-mer began to jump up and down, waving her spear and shouting loudly. All the girls followed her example. Together, they looked like a pretty confident pack of dangerous animals. At least, the bears seemed to think so. Both the mother and cub paused and sniffed the air again. The cub settled back on its haunches and let its mother take the lead.

The giant mother swayed her head back and forth in seeming indecision, then moved forward again. Suh-mer shouted all the louder, then reached down and snatched up a large stone. As the bear approached the edge of the camp, she threw it hard. The others also threw stones. Two of the rocks hit the bear. They couldn't have hurt much, but again, she hesitated.

Suddenly, from behind, Rah-hain shouted loudly. A pack of four huge hyenas had broken through the other side of the camp. They ran straight past Rah-hain and toward the meat surrounded by the fire pits. The bears saw the hyenas taking advantage of their hesitancy and both came barreling in for their share of the spoils.

Rocks were flying, and spearheads were slashing. Hyenas were snarling, and bears were roaring. In the middle of it all, a dog was barking, and men were shouting.

Then, it was over. The hyenas took off in one direction, while the bears lumbered off in another. The women then turned toward the strange men-like creatures and backed up, raising their spears.

“Hey, hey!” Dave said putting his taser in his belt and lowering his spear. “We were just trying to help.”

Joe followed Dave’s example and raised his hands to show he meant no harm. But Dean kept his taser in hand.

Soo-sahn took one step toward them, partially lowering her spear. “Thank you for your help. We would have lost much of our meat.”

“Oh, my goodn…!” Dean gasped out in disbelief. “It can *talk*!”

Soo-sahn raised her spear a bit higher. “You are welcome to stay in the outer edge of our camp until our men return. Brah-heez will get you something to eat and drink.” With that, Rah-hain came to keep an eye on the men, while the others went back to work tending the fires and the meat.

Laika walked with her tail wagging over to Brah-heez. “Look at this baby wolf, Mommy,” the young girl giggled. “It’s all curly and cute.”

“That’s not a wolf,” Suh-mer corrected. “That’s a dog. Many people in the cities keep them. But I’ve never seen one that looks like this one.”

"Why don't we have a dog?" Brah-heez asked, putting down some meat and water for Laika.

"We don't need one on the ice," her mother answered. "It would just be another mouth to feed."

Dean was still locked in a state of disbelief as he listened to the two interact. All he could do was stare at them with his mouth partially open.

Joe leaned forward a bit and smiled at Rah-hain. "Has anyone in your family seen someone dressed like us, only with dark skin?"

Rah-hain shook her head slowly. "What happened to your eyes? And your nose?" she asked.

Joe smiled again. "Well, where I come from, all the people have eyes and noses like mine."

"Why are you all so tall?" Rah-hain asked. "Do you come from the land of the giants?"

Suh-mer shushed her daughter. "It is rude to ask so many questions. They cannot help the way they look."

"We are hoping your men have seen our dark friend," Dave said eagerly. "When do you expect them back?"

Suh-mer looked at the sky. "Not before sunset, unless they make a good kill."

Joe and Dave looked at Dean who shook his head. In a cool tone he replied, "We can't wait that long. Come on, we have to get back to our own camp before it gets dark.

"Don't go, please!" Soo-sahn said suddenly. She stopped working and hurried over to stand in front of the men. "My Tah-hom must meet you!"

Dean raised his taser and asked suspiciously, "*Why* are you so eager for us to meet him?"

Soo-sahn looked back at Suh-mer. "Remember what I told you? Jah-hon and Jah-himmy both said they saw the *Lord's star*. Maybe…"

"The *Lord's star*?" Dean asked, taking two steps back. A look of both confusion and fear filled his face. "What are you talking about?"

Soo-sahn also took two steps back. She, too, seemed suddenly afraid. "You aren't people from the west are you? You do believe in the Lord, don't you?"

Joe and Dave both looked at Dean, expecting him to answer. But he just stood there staring at her.

Finally, Joe answered, "We have traveled from far away. But, we have set up our camp just a short distance to the east."

"But," Whin-die, who had now also stopped working, asked, "do you believe in the one true God, or in the many false gods of the pagans?"

Joe and Dave again looked at Dean, but he purposely tightened his lips, refusing to answer. So, Dave answered, "Yes, we believe in the one true God who lives in heaven."

All the women relaxed again, and Soo-sahn smiled excitedly. "Then, maybe you are the help sent to us from the Lord."

Dave opened his mouth to reply to this strange comment but was interrupted by Laika as she growled and moved in front of Rah-hain as if to protect her from whatever was approaching. The women all ran to their piles of stones and grabbed up their spears. The three men took out their tasers.

Then, after a tense moment of waiting, a shrill whistle filled the air. All the women dropped their spears and cheered, then hurried over to the far side of the camp. Joe and Dave put their tasers away so that they would not appear threatening. Dean lowered his, but kept it in his hand.

Three short burly men appeared through the grass. Each had at least 150 pounds of raw meat strapped to his back. They came in talking and smiling, but stopped short when they saw the three strangely dressed men on the other side of the camp.

Suh-mer talked quickly to the tallest of the men. "These strange men helped us to save our meat from two bears and a pack of hyenas. And, they have weapons that seem to be able to hurt from a distance without throwing anything. But, they have not harmed us. They believe in the true God."

Soo-sahn nodded to the most powerfully built of the three, and added, "They say that they are from very far away, but are camped not far to the east."

Tah-hom stopped halfway across the camp to take the meat off his back. Then, he walked over to the three strangers. He was very short in comparison, but he probably weighed as much as, or more than, any of them.

"He's a Neanderthal," Dean said out loud.

Tah-hom looked up at Dean. "No, I am a Cle-ahn-tur, as were my father and my mother. What are you?"

"Me? Well…I'm a *Homo sapiens*." Dean replied with a tinge of pride slipping into his tone.

"Humph," Tah-hom said, "I've not heard of them. Strange that you would speak our language so well when you're from some unknown people group." Then, he turned to Dave and Joe. "And, what are your friends?"

"They are also *Homo sapiens*," Dean answered.

"No way!" Tah-hom looked surprised. "They don't look anything like you." After a pause, he concluded, "I guess only one of their parents was one of those *Homo sapien* folks."

Dean looked a little offended, but Dave and Joe busted out laughing. That was enough to set Tah-hom to laughing, too. "Well, whatever you all are, you're welcome in our camp."

"Thank you, sir," Joe answered heartily.

"You're welcome," Tah-hom smiled. "But, my name's not *sir*. It's Tah-hom."

"Hey!" Dave stepped forward. "My dad's name is Tom!"

"Then, he must be a good man," Tah-hom laughed again.

With this, even Dean seemed to relax. And all three of the "*Homo sapiens*" went forward to help the "Neanderthals" cut up their meat and set it on the wires to cook or to be dried for later use.

After an hour's hard work, Joe, Dean, and Dave sat a little ways off from the others and discussed whether they should head back to the ship or camp with Tah-hom and Wah-ulf's families. Tah-hom had advised against going back east. He said that they had met another hunting party who had heard that a family of mega-mouth dragons had recently moved into the area. Three men would be no match for a pair of mega-mouths. Although these large dragons were now quite rare, everyone still knew that fire was the best defense against a mega-mouth.

"Tom's group is heading out in a day or two, anyway—as soon as this last load dries. Why don't we wait and travel with them?" Joe suggested. "That way, we can pull their meat for them, and we'll all be on hand if a mega-mouth shows up—whatever a mega-mouth is."

"I hope we don't find out," Dave said in all seriousness.

"No," Dean shook his head. "We can't let them see our rovers and cameras. Who knows how it might mess up their evolutionary progression. And, we can't let them slow us down. Besides, they might try to steal things from us."

Dave stood up with a scowl on his face and demanded, "What is your problem?"

"No!" Dean responded. "What's *your* problem? You've lost all objectivity. Our job is not to help a bunch of sub-human Neanderthals. Our job is to find John and get back to Earth!"

Now Joe stood up, too, "Subhuman Neanderthals? Talk about losing 'objectivity.' I think I hear a hint of prejudice coming out of your mouth."

Dean paused, trying to regain his scientific composure. "You are being ridiculous! Neanderthals aren't even human. How can I be prejudice against something that's not even a person?"

Joe seemed stunned to hear his captain talk in such a way. "What are you saying?" he spread out his hands. "That, just because these folks look different from anyone we've seen before, they aren't people?"

Dave looked over at Suh-mer who was using some antler tips to comb through Wah-ulf's long hair, preparing to re-braid it after having rinsed the dirt and blood out of it. "Nobody's gonna tell me that they aren't people!"

"Look!" Dean sighed. "As far as we can tell, Planet T-3 is mirroring Earth's evolutionary history. If that's true, then these, well, these creatures are not really human. It will be tens of thousands of years before the first real humans appear."

Joe watched as Whin-die and Brah-heez teased Laika into begging for a scrap of meat. "So, what's keeping them from being human?" Joe asked.

Dean looked a little uncertain and defensive, but answered, "Science would say it is *time*. But, as a Christian, I would say it is the *soul* that's missing."

Dave rolled his eyes and snorted, "How do you know they don't have a soul? One of the first things the women talked to us about was God."

Dean looked frustrated. "Yeah, I know. I'm not sure I fully understand that. But, look, God used evolution to create the world, right? Then, at some point, a group of human-like animals evolved into just what God wanted. And, He put a soul into these people—it's…the soul that sets us apart from the animals."

As Dean talked, Laika came running over to Joe and lay down at his feet. Joe stooped to pat her for a moment, and when he stood back up, he seemed to have come to an important conclusion. "Chief," he said, "I have never wanted to push my personal beliefs about God on others. But, I have to tell you, I can't believe that God would work things out in such a lame way that good, caring people—like these Neanderthals—wouldn't have souls!"

"Well," Dean fumbled, "I guess, maybe, God could be doing it differently here on T-3."

"Why?" Dave scoffed. "Because He didn't do it right the first time? You keep saying God is perfect. Well, if He's so perfect, I wouldn't think He would have to *try again* because He didn't like the way things turned out the first time."

Dean was opening his mouth to defend himself when Laika's nose went straight up into the air. Everyone paused. She stood up and sniffed again. Then, she began to shake with excitement. She jumped up to lick Joe's face, then, with two small woofs, she raced out of camp and into the tall grass.

CHAPTER 9

"Well," John said as he climbed out of the rover, "our battery is getting low. I guess we'd better give it some time to recharge." Looking toward the late afternoon sun, he asked Jah-hon, "How much farther do you think before we get to your parents' camp?"

"The family we passed said it was half a day's walk. We've come at least that far. So, I guess it should be close. I can't figure out why we haven't seen the smoke from their fires."

As they all scanned the horizon, something charged out of the nearby grass and flung itself, full-strength, onto John, knocking him to the ground. Jah-hon had his spear raised and ready to plunge when he realized that John was not screaming in terror, but in joy.

"Laika, my best girl! Where have you been? And where are the others?" John asked as he hugged the dog and rubbed her long, silky ears.

"What kind of animal is that?" Tah-hommy said, peeking out from behind Jah-him.

"I think it's some sort of a long-haired dog," Jah-hon answered. "Anyway, they obviously know each other."

Then, they all heard thumping and crashing sounds approaching through the tall grass. Everyone got behind the rover and reached for their spears. But Laika bounced and yipped excitedly. So, John dropped his spear and ran toward the grass, unable to wait for his crewmates to get to him.

The crew was reunited in a giant bundle of a hug, laughing and talking all at once, while Laika ran in ecstatic circles around them.

Before this reunion was over, Tah-hom, Wah-ulf, and Tah-him broke out of the tall grass with their spears raised.

"Daddy!" Tah-hommy shouted and ran to hug his father. Then, a whole different reunion started.

After that, there were introductions and explanations. Finally, the serious discussion began. "Dad," Jah-hon said, "I doubled checked everything, and it looks like the big thaw you were worried about might be starting."

"But, Jah-hon," Wah-ulf said, "you weren't even supposed to check on the Vast West Wall until today."

"That's right," Jah-hon answered. "Our new friend, John, has a rover. It's kind of like the horses or camels grandfather says they ride in the big cities, only it's not alive." He stopped and pointed back at the recharging rover. "And, it rolls on wheels."

While the three Neanderthals examined John's rover and asked questions, Laika again began to sniff the air. She went to Joe and nudged his hand. "What's wrong, girl?" he asked, giving her a pat. She nudged him again and looked to the west.

Tah-hom had stopped talking and was watching Laika. He followed her gaze to the west. "That is the direction of our camp. I think we'd better head back."

Leaving the rover to recharge, the group headed along the now-obvious path through the tall grass. About halfway back to the camp, they began to feel what was making Laika nervous. The ground was making strange vibrations…"Boom, booom, boooom." Then came a blasting high-pitched roar, which seemed to be answered by an even louder blast.

"Hurry!" Tah-hom shouted. "The mega-mouths have found our camp!"

Although the crew of the Discovery, with their longer legs, could have passed the others up, they held back, uncertain of what they would find in front of them. When they broke into the circular camp, each woman and girl already held a large flaming stick in one hand and a spear in the other. Without a word, the men and boys ran to the piles of rocks and spears. John, Joe, and Dave had their tasers in one hand and their spears in another.

Only Dean hesitated. Something deep inside of him told him that this very well might be a fight to the death. Once again, he could see the face of his dear Susi. How could he risk his chances of returning to her just to save the food supply of some half-human creatures? He started to call back the other crewmembers but knew they wouldn't listen to an order to retreat. So, taking a few steps back, he crouched down in the grass and waited to see what was coming.

"Boom, boooom!" the ground shook. Then, it appeared. In form, it was a *T. rex*, straight out of Jurassic Park. However, its color was strikingly different. It was a deep bluish-green with yellow tiger stripes from its nose to its tail. Only its yellow belly and undersides were without stripes. If it hadn't been so terrifyingly huge, Dean would have thought that it looked ridiculous. Four more gigantic steps brought the head of the beast to the edge of the camp.

Everyone shouted and jumped, flashing their fire-sticks. The *T. rex* leaned in closer, smelling an easy meal. Only the heat from the fires held it back. Shaking its nearly six-foot-long head in frustration, the mega-mouth screamed another long blast at the little shouting people and their fire-sticks.

Then, straightening up, it began to circle around to the other side of the camp.

Dean saw he was about to be trapped, and panicked. Standing up, he turned to run away through the tall grass, but suddenly, Laika was in front of him. She barked and wouldn't let him past. When he tried to jump over her, she nipped at his legs and grabbed hold of his pants, tugging and growling. Getting hold of her, Dean tossed her aside and kept running. But, Laika ran with him and kept trying to block his path.

"Rrrrroooooaarrrr!" Suddenly, the tall grass split open in front of Dean, revealing a second mega-mouth waiting in ambush. The beast stepped forward, trying to crush Dean. However, it was not very fast, and he jumped and rolled out of the way. Laika ran in circles and barked, nipping at any part of the dinosaur she could safely attack.

After trying in vain to smash the pesky dog, the mega-mouth ignored Laika and concentrated on Dean. Giant jaws snapped closed less than a yard behind Dean as he ran blindly through the tall grass. "Help, somebody help me!" he screamed as he tripped and fell.

"Boom, boooom," the *T. rex* stood above him. Turning its head sideways to look him over, it opened its mouth and shrieked its victory. Its mate answered with a roar from over by the camp. Dean looked up into the giant open mouth that was about to bring an end to his life. Then, seemingly out of nowhere, a large stone flew into the dinosaur's mouth and landed under its tongue.

Immediately, the *T. rex* began to violently shake its head. Then, it clawed at its mouth with its tiny forearms. Screaming and shrieking, it stumbled backward. Dean jumped up and turned to see Tah-hom close beside him. "It was a rock from the fire," Tah-hom explained. But, before Dean could reply, the ground began to shake. The other

T. rex was answering its mate's distress call and was upon them almost instantly.

Tah-hom held up a long spear and stepped in front of Dean. With a powerful thrust, the spearhead went into the soft under part of the *T. rex's* jaw. It roared in pain and raised itself high into the air, taking Tah-hom with it. Shaking its head, it clawed at the Neanderthal with its small forearms. Finally, Tah-hom was ripped off and thrown aside. By this time, the others had come with spears, rocks, and tasers. Bombarded from all sides, both mega-mouths turned and retreated.

Joe and one half of the group turned and ran back to guard the camp. Dean and the others ran to where Tah-hom lay twisted and bleeding in the grass. Soo-sahn took her husband's head into her lap and began to weep. Little Tah-hommy hid behind his mother and sobbed.

Dave put his hand over his mouth and ran away into the endless weeds.

Dean knelt beside Tah-hom. Taking hold of his hand, he trembled. Tah-hom's hands were burned raw from holding the scorching hot rock. "Why?" he asked. "Why would you do this for me?"

Tah-hom turned his head to look into Dean's face. Then, even through his pain, he smiled. "Dean, you must know… my great-grandfather told my grandfather, who in turn told my father, who then told me, 'It is God's will that you must love one another. And, this is love, that one is willing to lay down his life for another.'"

Dean replied, "And there is no greater love than this, that a man lay down his life for a friend."

"So," Tah-hom nodded, "you *do* know."

Dean wiped the tears from his face, then answered, "Yes. And, now I also know that—although I'm not worthy—you are my true friend."

Dave came rushing back among them with a medium-sized metal box in his hand. Taking out two bottles of cleansing solution, he handed one to Dean, while he used the other to begin preparing Tah-hom's larger wounds for stitching. He handed Soo-sahn a small oxygen mask and told her to hold it over her husband's face. Then, he gave little Tah-hommy a tube of antibiotic to smear onto some of his father's bad scrapes.

****

"You know," Billy smiled as he leaned back against the cave wall, "it's a great compliment to any storyteller when he can get his audience to cry."

"Who's crying?" Mark asked, pulling a guilty hand down from his cheek.

"I sure am," Tasha said through shameless tears. "I'm so glad that Dean realized that Tah-hom was as much a person as he was."

Dr. Chen cleared his throat, and added in a husky voice, "In some ways, I'd say that he was *more* of a person…"

"You're more right than you realize," Billy said seriously. "Modern evolutionary beliefs, and all those magazine covers, and museum dioramas, and all those movies with actors dressed up like hairy half-humans have brainwashed us to see 'prehistoric' man *backwards*."

"What do you mean?" Dr. Chen asked. And, everyone leaned forward to hear Billy's answer.

But Darin raised his hand excitedly. "Oh, I know. Can I tell? I know. Let me tell."

Billy laughed and waved the 'floor' to Darin. "My voice needs a break." So, without a word, everyone turned their attention to Darin.

"It's like this," Darin began. "In the beginning, God made Adam and then Eve. He made them *perfect*. And, God's *perfect* is a whole lot more perfect than we realize. People like to picture Adam and Eve as innocent little kids who walked around picking flowers all day. But, that's ridiculous!" Darin scoffed. "When God made people, He made them in His very own image. He made them to be *GREAT*. And, He gave them an immense task—to rule over the entire created world, starting with the Garden of Eden." Here, Darin stood up to emphasize his point. "If you spend some time really thinking about what's involved in ruling over an entire world—even a perfect world, you'll realize that it's not a job for a simpleton. Nope! God gave Adam and his perfect partner, Eve, a huge, challenging, exciting, majorly humongous job. Why?"

Mark guessed, "Was it because they were supposed to live forever, so they needed a really big job?"

Darin looked impressed and nodded. "Well, that's part of it. But, I think it was also because God had made Adam and Eve that *GREAT*. Physically, Adam and Eve were strong and in perfect health—like LeBron James, Serena Williams, and Derek Jeter all rolled into one. And, intellectually, Adam and Eve must have not only been Einsteins, but also Rembrandts, Handels, and Marie Curies, too. Do you see what I'm saying?" Darin looked around the cave. Everyone nodded in an amazed silence.

"Okay, but now, we need to go a little deeper," Darin said. "We need to go beyond physical, intellectual, emotional, and even artistic. We need to go into their very genetic make-up. Remember, they were *perfect*—made perfect by *Mr. Perfection* Himself, God. Anything we can think of that would be genetically good is not half as good as God made them. I mean, think about it…God knew what they would need, not just for when they were created, but forever, on down through generation after generation after generation. And, He knew what they would need if and when they fell into sin, and the world was no longer such a wonderful place."

David raised his hand. "You're forgetting something else important. Before Adam and Eve sinned, God used to physically walk with them through the Garden. And, while they were walking together, I'll bet they talked about all kinds of incredible things, like—What makes the plants grow? What are the stars made of? Why does the sun set…?"

"Maybe even," Aaron jumped in, "what's the molecular make-up of the human genome…?"

Billy chuckled, "You know, anything's possible. God knew the answers to everything, and Adam and Eve had the intellectual capacity to understand it all. And, you school kids need to realize, this was not some boring brain-cruncher that Adam and Eve had to drag through each evening. No. This was the joy of their lives. They were made like sponges, eager to learn, explore, understand, excel, and conquer."

"Wow!" Dr. Chen just took it all in.

"But," Darin took back his audience, "the big point here is this—Mankind did *not* simply and slowly progress forward like evolution, and the magazine covers, and the movies say. No! That's all part of what evolutionists *assume* to be true. But, if we take the biblical viewpoint, it's just the opposite."

Dr. Chen looked both excited and frustrated. "So, what are you getting at?"

Darin sighed. "See, it's so obvious, but all of evolution's brainwashing has made you—and everyone—so blind.

"It's like this," he continued. "God made people perfect. It wasn't until *after* the Fall that things started to fall apart. Do you see what I mean? Genetic weakness, harmful mutations, learning disabilities, asthma, high cholesterol, cancer…these all came into play *after* the Fall."

Dr. Chen shook his head. "I think I get what you're saying—that people started perfect and are getting steadily worse, instead of getting steadily better (as evolution claims). But, that just doesn't work. I mean, just look at Billy's story.

We have cavemen walking around using spears, and we have modern men driving rovers and using tasers."

Billy took over. "What you're saying is an historical fact that is backed up by all the artifacts anyone has ever dug up. However, *technology* doesn't necessarily prove *progress*. Look at ancient Egypt, or China, or the ancient Mayan cultures. These peoples made colossal pyramids, invented intricate written languages, even made temples to such exact specifications that the moonlight would only pass through a specific window on one—and only one—day each year." Billy paused. "And, just think, they did all this *without* modern technology, and *without* computers. I'd say that they were some pretty smart and able folks."

"So, then why were they living in caves, and tents, and running around half-naked in mammoth skins?" Mark questioned.

Sarah spoke up. "Not all of them lived in caves. In Billy's story, there were people who lived in cities, too."

"Yep," Aaron said. "There's all kinds of archeological evidence that shows people lived advanced lives in the cities. They had shops that sold food and clothes, produced and sold paintings, and made jewelry. They also had real money—like gold, silver, or jewels. But besides that, they had things of little value that represented money—like seashells."

"You mean, they used seashells like we use paper money now?" Sarah asked.

"Sometimes," Billy smiled. "Mark, the people who lived in caves and wore clothes made of skins most likely did so because they were using all their time and energy just surviving tough times as they forged forth into new frontiers. Think about the pioneers who settled the western parts of the United States. The men spent their days hunting, farming, and caring for their animals. The women cooked, cleaned, and cared for the children. They lived simple and basic—not because they couldn't do any better, but because that was the *smartest* way for them to live in their situation at the time."

"Okay, okay." Dr. Chen held up his hands. "I think I need a break. My head's spinning. I've got too many questions. Like, why are there so many, many fossils if the earth is only 6,000 years old? And, if Noah's Flood was really a worldwide flood, how did all the animals fit into his ark? And, if nothing ate meat before the Fall, why do so many animals have such sharp teeth? And, finally, here's the stumper my agnostic brother hit our pastor with—if the Bible is literally true, where in the world did Cain get his wife?"

Billy slapped Dr. Chen on the shoulder. "I know it can all seem pretty overwhelming. But, don't worry, there are answers to all your questions. We'll talk it all through on the ship."

CHAPTER 10

Tying all their coats together, Dave, Dean, John, and Joe slowly, and very gently, put Tah-hom on the makeshift gurney. Then, everyone helped to move him back to the circular camp with its protective fires. Dean examined Tah-hom and found a broken arm and some fractured ribs. He feared a punctured lung.

"We have to get him out of this open land," Dave insisted. "There are just too many big critters that are after the winter meat."

Dean nodded grimly. "John, I'm gonna put you in charge of coming up with the most comfortable way of transporting Tah-hom. Dave, you and the other men need to come up with a way to pull all this meat by rover power."

Dean turned to the women, "You ladies need to prepare the meat for travel. And, tonight, we'll need you to make a couple of days' worth of easily eaten soup for Tah-hom to eat along the way. He'll need lots of liquids and plenty of nourishment. I'm gonna start him on some oral antibiotics right now—that's a special medicine that will protect his wounds from infection. Then, he'll need all the rest he can get tonight before we head out in the morning."

"I think we should build several smaller fires near the outsides of the camp," Wah-ulf suggested. "That will be a greater deterrent to the animals that go hunting at night. It will free us up from guard duty and give us more time to get things ready for the morning."

At Soo-sahn's suggestion, everyone gathered around Tah-hom and prayed. As they finished, Jah-him told his father, "See, Dad, I told you that Jah-hon and I had seen the *Lord's star*. Do you see how these men have come to help us?"

Tah-hom smiled up at his son. "Jah-himmy, the Lord's star does not come to help one man, or one man's family. No, the *Lord's star* is a sign to the masses. It is a sign that salvation is coming to many, many people."

****

After a long and busy night, the group left camp just after sunrise the next morning. One of the rovers had been taken apart and the parts used to make two trailers. The two trailers were attached to two of the rovers. Tah-hom was laid out on one of the trailers, with Soo-sahn and Dean taking turns making sure that he was safe and comfortable. The other trailer was loaded with supplies and some of the dried meat.

The fourth rover pulled the sled that was piled high with most of the meat and skins gathered during the week of hunting.

Everyone took turns walking and riding and driving. But still, the group was not quite halfway back to the family cave before sundown. After holding a brief meeting, it was decided that they should travel as long as the rovers had power. Then, they would have to wait for the sun to rise enough to recharge their 'mechanical donkeys.' Those who were walking each carried a spear and a torch. Rocks were gathered in small piles on the trailers in case they were attacked.

Numerous hungry eyes followed the group through the night, but none seemed willing to attack such a large 'pack' of people. So, the group made it to the halfway mark before their rovers gave out. Exhausted, they set up guard shifts and then slept on tree-horn skins until nearly noon the next day. By that time, the rovers were ready to roll again.

It was evening when they finally reached the cave on the ice. Everyone cheered. Finally, they were able to carefully carry Tah-hom up the steep hill that led to the family cave. Tah-him and Jah-hon went ahead of the others and chased away two young knife-cats.

Then, all fifteen crowded into the cave. Tah-him started a fire, while Dean and Soo-sahn tried to get Tah-hom comfortable. Everyone set things in order—the biggest task being to bury the hundreds of pounds of meat five feet into a nearby ice-den. Then, they ate and laid side-by-side and slept until the sun was high the next day.

Only Wah-ulf was up with the sun. Gathering a few supplies, he woke Jah-hon and John and said they needed to go check on the Vast Wall. So, they slipped and slid down the hill to the waiting rovers.

John let Jah-hon do the driving while he looked through some of the supplies to see if there would be any useful tools for their day by Green Lake.

Halfway there, Wah-ulf turned to Jah-hon. "Something is not right. I have not seen one woolly elephant or rhino. And, all the birds and small dragons keep circling around above the lake."

"Stop the rover," John said suddenly. "Now turn it off." John jumped out with a small flat box in his hand. Laying it flat on the ice, he watched its digital numbers. Then, he ran 100 feet toward the mountain and did the same thing. Then he ran another 100 feet. Finally, he called for Jah-hon to start the rover and come ahead.

As they drove along, John explained, "This box reads the vibrations of the ground. In another couple of minutes, I'll check again. But, from what I could see, the underground vibrations are getting stronger as we get closer to Green Lake."

No one said anything for the next five minutes. They knew the serious implications of what John had said. Then, John had them stop again, and he put the box back on the ground. He ran ahead three more lengths, then called for the others to come get him. "Wolf," he said, "look at these numbers. See, this '*4*' is like four marks. This '*6*' is six marks. Those are from our first stop. Look here, this '*15*' is fifteen marks, and the next is '*22*'. The vibrations are definitely getting stronger the closer we get to the mountain lake."

"Could it just be a shift that will soon settle?" Jah-hon asked hopefully.

"We can't be sure," Wah-ulf said. "The birds and animals seem to be taking it very seriously. We'll have to go up and see for ourselves. However, no matter what, I think we will have to send out a warning for everyone to move out of here and to pass it along to everyone as they move out of the danger zone."

"How many people are involved?" John asked.

Wah-ulf shook his head, "Many hundreds at least, probably thousands. Tah-hom's family lives down south, and he says that there are two smaller cities and one large city within a day's walk of his family's home. And, who knows how many more live within reach of the immeasurable amount of water locked up in that lake?"

Pulling the rover up to the lowest point of the icy walls that held back the lake, the three men scaled the mountain as quickly as possible. At the top, Wah-ulf told John and Jah-hon to wait where they were. Then, he ran out onto the Vast Wall. He was not there for more than a few minutes before he came running back. He did not stop, but ran past them and started down the mountain. The other two followed with fear welling up inside of them.

Once they were in the rover, Wah-ulf said, "I cannot believe it has not yet burst. There is no time. We will have to leave immediately for the north."

"But what about the thousands to the west and the south? They won't have anyone to warn them."

"It is very sad," Wah-ulf frowned. "But, there's nothing we can do—unless, you young men with no families to protect are willing to spread the warning. But, honestly, I think it would be a hopeless mission."

John spoke up, "Dean said that Tah-hom shouldn't be moved for at least a week. He has lost a lot of blood and is very weak."

Wah-ulf looked torn. There just didn't seem to be an obvious answer. Jah-hon and John thought of several ideas, but as soon as they started to suggest them, the idea would sink beneath an obvious flaw.

But, before they reached home, John had a sudden thought. "Wolf," he asked, "would this side of the Green Lake Mountain be safe if we could get the lake to drain out on the east side?"

Wah-ulf took time to think it through. "From what I know about the layout of the land to the east, Green Lake would drain into uninhabited land both to the east and to the south." But then he shook his head. "The problem is that the East Wall of Green Lake is nearly four times as thick as the West Wall. There is no way for us to weaken it in time."

"I have an idea," John said. "But, I'll have to talk it over with Dean, Dave, and Joe."

****

Back at the cave, the men and women discussed the emergency and John's idea.

"We can spare the extra fuel cell," Joe said, "but we won't be able to land again, nor will we be able to do the post-take off aerial survey NISA has scheduled."

"NISA will just have to live with it," Dave said. "Anyway, we got lots of pictures during the pre-landing survey."

John added, "I'll be satisfied as long as we have enough extra fuel to turn back and do a fly over to make sure everyone's okay on Tah-hom's side of the wall."

Dean shook his head. "I'm afraid we can't even spare that much fuel."

John started to protest, but Tah-hom lifted a weak hand and spoke. "My friend, I understand your desire, but I think perhaps it is better for you to simply do all you can do and be gone. You can only entrust our well-being to God."

The Discovery crew knew that Tah-hom was right, but they didn't even want to consider that their mission might fail.

So, after a moment's silence, they turned their attention to planning the project. Jah-hon and Jah-him were sent to ask the other two nearby families to come and help. Cranes, and pulleys, and a giant sled, and much more had to be constructed before they could even get their giant 'bomb' to the East Wall.

After nearly three days of non-stop, backbreaking work, they were ready. Working together, they all loaded the 'surplus' fuel cell and began to pull it toward the east side of the mountain lake. There, it was pulled and pushed and towed up the mountain side and embedded deep into the icy wall.

The mission took the entire day. That night, the group talked around a large fire. Tah-hom was able to sit partially up, and his wounds were healing well. There was now little fear of infection. And Dean had declared both of Tah-hom's lungs to be strong and healthy. His arm would take several more weeks to heal, but it was set straight and should be fine. Everyone was thankful.

As they ate dinner, Jah-him looked up at Joe. "When you break the East Wall, it will seem like the days of my great-grandfather—the days of the Great Disaster."

"Of course," Tah-hom spoke up, "in great-grandpa Jah-eff-ahth's day, the waters covered the whole earth, and all but eight people were killed. This time will be comparatively small. And, because the Lord has sent His help, we can hope that no human life will be lost."

At hearing this, Dean had a sudden revelation and jumped up so fast that he hit his head on a low part of the cave ceiling. But he was too excited to care. "Your great-grandpa Japheth? Do you mean Japheth, the son of Noah and the brother of Shem and Ham?"

"Yes," Tah-hom answered. "Of course, we are all related to Noe-ah."

"You knew Noah?" Dean asked in astonishment.

Tah-hom laughed. "Well, no, I'm afraid I'm not *that* old. However, one of my father's uncle's actually ate in Noe-ah's home on occasion. He even saw for himself the written accounts of our forefathers from the times before the Great Disaster."

John was almost in shock. "So, this Great Disaster you keep talking about was actually Noah's Flood?"

Soo-sahn looked a little uncertain. "Is that what your people call it? The Great Disaster was when the Lord God looked down on the evil wickedness of all the people and decided to destroy them and all living creatures with a giant Flood that covered even the highest mountains. However, our great ancestor, Noe-ah, found favor in God's eyes. So, his family was chosen to take two of every land creature into a very large boat. And, that was how a few people and animals were saved from God's anger. Now, these people and animals are refilling the earth with their children's children's children."

John sat forward and asked Tah-hom, "This *Great Confusion* you mentioned before, does that, by chance, have to do with the Tower of Babel?"

"Of course," one of the other neighbors nodded solemnly. "Many years after the Great Disaster, Noe-ah's descendants rejected God's command to spread throughout the world. They decided to stay all together in one big city. And, as we know, sin grows quickly in cities. Even though Noe-ah warned them not to defy God, they chose to do as they pleased. They told Noe-ah that they were so great that they were going to build a stairway to heaven. Then they would prove to everyone that they were just as great as God Himself."

"Man!" Dean rubbed the small bump on the top of his head. "I guess I never really thought it through—I mean, that Noah would still be alive during the times of the Tower of Babel."

"So," John continued the story, "because of the people's stubborn pride, God confused their languages. And, it all caused so much difficulty and confusion that the people gave up their tall tower and divided up and went to live in different parts of the world—just like God had originally commanded them to."

Jah-him spoke up, "I hope to one day be able to travel to your part of the world, where they have ships that can fly, rovers that can be driven, and cameras that draw perfect pictures."

Jah-hon reached over and scratched Laika's silky long ears. "I'd just want to get us a few good dogs."

"I'm afraid it's very, very far away," Joe sighed.

"And, for now," Dave added, "we'd better get some rest—tomorrow's a big day."

After the several days of hard work, everyone fell into a deep and heavy sleep. Some slept in the cave, others out under the starry sky. No one worried much about wild animals since they hadn't seen anything but birds for the past two days. All the animals seemed to have fled the area after the warning tremors had started. Besides, Laika was with them, always on the alert.

As Dean slept under a warm mammoth fur, Susi came to him in a dream. His heart swelled with joy at seeing the bride of his youth. Without a word, she took him by the hand and led him to the bench he had built for her under their favorite shade tree. It was strange because they seemed to be still on the icy glacier *and* in their warm Florida backyard at the same time. Holding hands, they silently looked at the stars together.

Then, Susi turned to her husband and put her warm hand up to his dirty, scruffy cheek. Her eyes 'spoke' how much she loved him. Standing up, she turned to look toward the Vast West Wall that held back the lake waters. "Dear Dean," she said without looking away from the high wall, "remember what Jesus tells us, 'Greater love has no one than this, that he lay down his life for his friends.'"

Dean felt fear and uncertainty rising in him. He tried to reach out and touch Susi, but his hand went right through her, and she continued looking toward the wall without moving. Suddenly, the wall cracked. Every hair on Dean's head stood on end. He reached again for Susi, yelling for her to run…

With a gasp, Dean was sitting up. Laika was licking his ear and wriggling her body around him. She was shaking with fear. Dean stood up and turned toward the mountain. His heart seemed to stop within him. Even from where he stood by Tah-hom's cave, he could see the West Wall was beginning to bulge out of shape.

There was no time. The wall was ready to rupture at any moment. Perhaps he should wake everyone, and they could run to the north. He put his trembling hands to his face, then turned to wake his friends in the cave. But, he stopped before entering. Tah-hom lay sleeping closest to the low-burning fire. His face was pale and his eyes were hollow in the fire light. Dean knew all too well why Tah-hom was in this weakened state—it was because of Dean's own foolishness. And he could see that there was no way Tah-hom could escape to the north. Dean knew there was only one option left. Turning back toward the Vast Wall, the peace of God came upon him as he set his mind to do it.

Dean reached down to pat Laika. He sat her down by Joe and told her firmly to *stay*, then turned to begin his silent descent from the cave. He walked as quietly as his boots would allow until he had gone a couple hundred feet to the southeast. He then began to run his race against the coming disaster. Several minutes later he had reached the only rover that had not been dismantled for project parts. Starting the engine, he set his goals—get to the ship to retrieve a detonator, then make it back to the *east* side of the mountain before the *West* Wall ruptured.

****

All the people at the cave continued to sleep soundly until an earsplitting explosion shocked everyone to their feet. The ground began to rumble and shake. Tah-hommy was knocked to the ground and cried out for his mother. Wah-ulf and Joe ran into the cave to carry Tah-hom away from the danger of falling rocks as the earthquake intensified. The men turned to face the bulging West Wall, waiting for the tide of death to come upon them and their families. The women huddled together and prayed for God's strength to face the fear and pain the flood would bring.

For several minutes, the ground continued to tremble and shake, but the bulging wall did not split. Then, Dave called out above the roaring noise that filled the air, "Look! Look to the southeast!"

Sliding down from the cave entrance, the men ran to the edge of the ice. It was clear that the noise was coming from that direction. But they couldn't tell what was happening. It seemed the whole eastern landscape was alive and moving, yet it continued to look the same.

Suddenly, Wah-ulf leaped into the air and shouted, "Praise the Living God! It's the lake! It's the lake draining out the east side!"

People began to hug and weep and laugh all at the same time. Only Laika did not join in the celebration. She trembled against Joe's legs and whined with her head low and her tail tucked. As Joe bent down to comfort her, he noticed that Dean wasn't in the small crowd. Standing up, he looked around, then ran over to Dave. "Hey, man!" he shouted over the noise of the flood, "Where's the Chief?"

Dave looked up toward the cave and saw a small group around Tah-hom, but Dean wasn't among them. He pointed to the southwest. "Maybe he went to the ship earlier to double check everything before today's liftoff."

Joe nodded, but neither of them believed Dean was in the ship.

Jah-hon and Wah-ulf joined Joe, John, and Dave as they ran to where the rover had been parked. "It's gone," Dave shouted to the others. And they all looked down in the dim dawn light to see the rover tracks heading toward to the southwest—toward the ship.

Everyone felt a surge of relief. Joe knelt down in the icy mud to hug Laika. "It's okay, girl," he said, trying to control his emotions. "Chief's okay. He's just at the ship." But Laika pulled away and whined. Then, she looked to the east and barked. John tried to pick her up, but she ran away from him. Looking to the east, she raised her nose and let out a pitiful yipping howl that sent shivers up everyone's back.

As they stood there, Wah-ulf ran up to them from the south. "There is another set of fresh rover tracks," he said in a sober voice. "They are heading back toward the East Wall."

CHAPTER 11

One week later, everyone, except for Tah-hom and Soo-sahn, walked with the Discovery crew to the edge of the ice. The crew members presented useful gifts to everyone—but nothing that would cause jealousy or disagreements among the good friends. (They had wisely decided that leaving advanced technology could eventually cause more harm than good.) Then, they said their final goodbyes and began their hike back to the ship—their rovers, along with many millions of dollars' worth of other NISA equipment, had been washed away in the flood.

Laika yipped and cried and kissed everyone goodbye, then ran to keep up with her crew.

Once everything was set and ready, Joe, John, and Dave launched the Discovery 2. As the landscape fell away beneath them, the crew was silent, all of them sorely conscious of Dean's empty seat.

On the ground below, Jah-hon watched the ship flash in the sunlight as it disappeared into the atmosphere. Turning around, he looked up at the icy wall that now surrounded a nearly empty lake bed and smiled. Indeed, the *Lord's star* had brought salvation to many people.

****

John's log:

Surviving birds are doing well. Surviving mammals are doing well. Hope they will survive our jump forward in time as we head back to the 21st century.

I've been thinking about how Jah-hon and generations of people before him have believed that seeing a star in the daytime would mean that God was going to send some sort of 'great help.' This is what I have concluded: Matthew 2:9: "After they [the Magi] had heard the king, they went on their way, and the star they had seen when it rose went ahead of them until it stopped over the place where the child [baby Jesus] was."

I believe God did use us (especially Dean) as a help for many people. But, I know that the 'ultimate' salvation has come to all mankind (past and future) through Jesus Christ.

****

Dave's log:

Reptiles and amphibians recovering. Several caged insect larvae have hatched after their parents died in the time-travel. I have put them into a moister atmosphere, hoping to increase their chances of surviving the time change.

T-3 is not a newly discovered planet. It is Earth. It is not entirely clear what caused our travel back in time. But the computers are indicating that the effect should be reversed in two days during the switchover to deceleration. We will let NISA figure out the logistics behind it all. It will be our task to share what we've

discovered and experienced during our visit into the past. And, it is our hearts' longing that it will turn the eyes of the world toward the living Creator.

****

Joe's log:

Lost very few plants while away from the ship.

I plan to name my firstborn son Dean. Dean followed in the footsteps of Jesus Christ—laying down his own life to save others. I pray to live as he did.

****

"The End," Billy said to the group around him.

No one argued or complained. Instead, they were quiet and thoughtful.

Darin was the first one to speak. "Man, Billy, that was your best story yet! I'm gonna name my first-born son *Dean*, too."

"I doubt it," Tasha smirked. "Bekah likes the name *Josiah*."

"*Josiah Dean* has a nice ring to it," David commented.

Mark stood up and shook his head. "I was hoping that Jah-hon would go forward in time with the Discovery crew."

"Duh!" Sarah said. "He couldn't go into the future. He had to stay behind and marry Whin-die,"

Aaron spoke up, "I thought Laika was gonna have some puppies they could leave with Jah-hon's family."

"I thought that, too!" Darin shot a dissatisfied glance in Billy's direction.

But Billy didn't notice, since Dr. Chen was saying in a frustrated tone, "I don't get it. What has turned so many of us, even Christians like myself, away from believing that the Bible is true?"

Darin, David, and Aaron looked at each and smiled. Together they answered with one of Darin's favorite catch phrases, "Media-mania!"

Billy explained, "For the past several decades, every form of media has been used to bombard people with evolution's millions and billions of years, slow and steady change, cavemen and missing links. And, it comes from every direction—public schools and colleges, books and newspapers, history museums and nature parks, television and movies, even children's cartoons teach evolution as *fact*. The problem is that many of the beliefs behind evolution are *not* compatible with what the Bible says. So, people have had to choose which one they are going to believe.

"Now, this is where the Church should be stepping in to assure and strengthen people's faith in the truth of God's Word. Unfortunately, many pastors and elders have themselves accepted evolution's lies.

"Now," Billy said sincerely, "it's not my job to judge these people. I myself was deceived for a time. No, we shouldn't judge our fellow Christians. Instead, we must educate them. God is pouring forth His wisdom on the creation scientists of today. He's opening up the mysteries of His creation in a way that shows that science truly does uphold the truth of the Bible."

****

As the group filed out of the cave, they paused among the rocks while Billy marked the cave entrance with a wooden cross he had formed by tying two large sticks together. Darin took down the exact GPS coordinates for the Coast Guard who would be called to come and collect Dean's remains to return them to his family for a proper burial.

Tasha wiped a tear from her eye. "I can't help but feel so sad knowing how much Susi must have missed her dear Dean."

Mark didn't like the lump rising in his own throat. "Oh, come on. This guy was probably nothing like the Dean in Billy's story.

Sarah took a hold of Tasha's hand. "Don't listen to him. I think maybe this real-life Dean was a lot like the Dean in Billy's story—maybe he even died saving a whole bunch of other people's lives."

Tasha smiled at her young friend and nodded. "I'll bet you're right."

****

The storm and cold of the day had given way to a balmy calm evening. All the slick ice had melted, leaving the rocks dark and damp. Everyone took in a deep breath of the fresh clean air, then headed carefully down to the shore. The dinghies had caught a lot of water but seemed in good shape. So, after contacting the ship, they bailed out the dinghies and pushed off from South Marble Island.

Once they were safely back aboard the *Scandinavian*, they were all glad to shower and change into dry clothes. Then they eagerly gathered around the snack bar.

"That's quite a little 'snack' you've got there." Billy laughed when he saw David's plate loaded with five lobster balls, four zucchini sticks, a pile of melon balls, crab toast, an apple, and several chocolate-covered strawberries.

"Hey!" David defended himself, "at least mine fits on one plate. Darin and Aaron both needed two."

Cory tapped David's shoulder and pointed toward one of the other tables. Big Aug looked up from his *three* plates and waved.

****

Dufthak spun around at the sound of Alrek's haunting scream. To his horror, he saw his friend suspended ten feet above the deck, wrapped in a giant rubbery arm covered with three-inch suction cups. Dufthak ran forward, fearlessly drawing his cutlass. He stabbed it deep into the Kratchan's tentacle. The arm shuddered, and Alrek was dropped onto the deck. But, almost instantly, two other tentacles appeared, snaking their way through the opposite railing. Each 30-foot arm felt blindly around for anything good to eat.

Dufthak's and Alrek's shouts brought Captain Joekull and Arngrim running to their aid. Jabbing and stabbing, the four sailors tried to convince the Kratchan that this meal wasn't worth the fight.

But then, beside the ship appeared a hideous sight. The giant squid had surfaced and was now viewing them with an eye nearly as big as they were tall. And four more tentacles appeared, closing in from all directions. Magnus and Dellingr came charging up from below deck armed with swords and a pistol. Dellingr was grabbed before he could even make a jab. He called to Magnus, "The eye…shoot that evil eye. It's our only chance."

Magnus staggered across the shaking ship's deck, closing in on the eye of the beast. When he was within ten feet of the ship's railing, the Kratchan focused its eye on him. Magnus recoiled at the intelligence he saw in its stare. For a moment, time stood still as man and beast faced each other down.

Then, Magnus raised his pistol. He could not hesitate or the ship, and the entire crew, would surely be lost. But, even as the pistol hammer pulled back, Magnus felt a leathery arm wrap itself around him. It lifted him high above the ship and began to squeeze the very life out of him. Magnus knew that he must not panic. He forced himself to concentrate and re-aim the pistol—his every nerve was focused on that awful, giant eye. Then, he again pulled back the hammer…

"Augie, are you out here?" a young woman's voice called from somewhere on the ship.

Captain Joekull and all his men stopped stabbing. The giant squid's tentacles stopped squeezing. And Magnus lowered his pistol to look around.

"Augie? Oh, there you are," Cory said with a chuckle. "Looks like you've got five of them pinned at the same time. Only Abel has managed to keep out of your reach."

"Hey, it's hardly fair," Darin complained from the bottom of the pile. "Big Aug says that wrestling is the only subject he ever got in an 'A' in."

Cory didn't show much sympathy, but she did stop to help David up. "Sorry little brother," she said as she put her arm through Aug's. "I'm afraid you guys will have to let Augustine beat you up another time. Right now, we're scheduled for a nice quiet walk to watch our last sunset on the *Scandinavian*."

Aaron, David, Jack, and Mark sighed, clearly disgusted. But Darin perked right up. "Hey, I'll bet Bekah would like to see the sunset, too." And, he was gone.

"Don't be too down, me maties," Abel encouraged in a perfect pirate's drawl. "Some day, it'll be your turn. Thou must see, it happens to the best of 'em. Ye may drive back the Jormangund. Ye may slaughter the Kratchan. But…in the end, ye too will fall—conquered, yes, conquered. And, by what, ye ask—by nothing more than a pretty face and a gentle hand." With that, he saluted them all and was off—looking for the pretty face and gentle hand of a young lass named Natasha.

"Humph!" Mark grumped. "Girls aren't good for anything!"

But, just then, his sister, Sarah, appeared. "Hey, you guys, Mrs. Carmen helped me make Titanic Tropical Treat Smoothies for you all!"

Mark looked at the others, then shrugged his shoulders. “Well, I guess I could be wrong.” Then, they were all running at high speed toward the snack bar.

A NOTE FROM DAVID

Hola Amigos,

You know, some Christians ask why I make such a big deal out of this 'creation stuff.' They think I should 'just focus on the Gospel.' So, I want to share something that really became clear to me through Billy's T-3 story.

You see, a lot of people run into big trouble when they start picking and choosing which parts of the Bible to believe. It starts like this: God didn't really create Adam and Eve in the Garden of Eden—since science says we evolved from apes. **Or:** 40 days of rain couldn't really have flooded the whole world—this is just a story to teach us some valuable lessons.

But, after a while, folks start saying things like: I don't think Jesus was really born of a virgin—that's just not scientific. And, the 'miracles' can probably be better explained by natural causes. And, the resurrection is just not medically believable.

In the end, it's like taking away the foundation of a building—one brick at a time—until the building collapses. Eventually, you're left with no Gospel at all. Science is so often used to tear down the truth of God's

Word—one brick at a time. But, creation science is showing that every part of the Bible is scientifically solid—giving a firm foundation that upholds the truth of the Gospel.

En la verdad de Dios,
David

ABOUT THE AUTHORS

John is a nationally certified middle school teacher. He has worked with teenagers for the past 20 years, both as a teacher and as a youth pastor. Lisa received her college degree in English Literature. She has also been active working with youth for the past 20 years. The Foxes live on a ten-acre farm in Central Ohio where they homeschool their six children. They also own lots of dogs and a variety of fun farm animals.

Authors' Note

Although this book is a work of fiction (unfortunately, we didn't really time-travel), the science and the historical theories behind the story are real. Scientific evidence supports the theory that there was *one* Ice Age a few thousand years ago following the Flood of Noah's day. And, strong scientific evidence also supports the theory that Neanderthals (*cavemen*) were as human as us. We believe the history of the Bible is true and that strong evidence supports this belief.

As always, we encourage our readers to ask questions and to do further research.

RECOMMENDED RESOURCES:

CREATION MAGAZINE

Keep your family informed on the latest easy-to-understand evidences for creation and against evolution! This unique full-color family magazine gives God the glory, refutes evolution, and gives you the answers to defend your faith. Exciting articles and great witnessing material you won't find anywhere else! Includes a beautifully illustrated full-color children's section in every issue. Arrives every three months!

EXPLORING GEOLOGY WITH MR. HIBB

This wonderfully illustrated, full-color book provides a biblical view of geology for elementary/primary school ages. It follows the entertaining adventures of the curious grasshopper, Mr Hibb, as he makes the learning of geology delightful and faith building.

ONE HUMAN FAMILY

A fascinating and deeply informative read that goes way beyond the normal 'all one race' conclusion. Combines sensitivity with a rejection of 'political correctness'. This blow-by-blow tour of race-related issues across the world is unlike any other creation book you've ever read. For many, it will make 'the lights go on'—not just about race but the whole biblical 'big picture' of human history.

WHAT THE SCHOOLS ARE TEACHING DVD

Have you ever wondered what textbooks are teaching about living things, as opposed to what the Bible teaches? It should not surprise you that they are opposites, but it might surprise you that the textbooks contain outright falsehoods. Learn to spot the lies so you can help your family, train up church youth, and answer the unbelieving world.

REFUTING EVOLUTION

Refuting Evolution is a hard-hitting critique of the most up-to-date arguments for evolution, to challenge educators, students, and parents. It is a powerful yet concise summary of the arguments against evolution and for creation. It will stimulate much discussion and help students and teachers think more critically about origins.

REFUTING EVOLUTION 2

This sequel comprehensively refutes arguments used to support evolution (as presented in TV documentaries and *Scientific American*). Read leading evolutionists in their own words, and then find straightforward answers from science and the Bible. *Refuting Evolution 2* will prepare you to answer the best arguments thrown at you by peers, teachers, neighbors, and skeptics.

CREATION.com

For more information on creation/evolution and Bible-science issues

AUSTRALIA
Creation Ministries International (Australia)
PO Box 4545
Eight Mile Plains, QLD 4113

Phone: (07) 3340 9888
Fax: (07) 3340 9889
ABN 31 010 120 304

CANADA
Creation Ministries International (Canada)
300 Mill St, Unit 7
Kitchener, ON N2M 5G8

Phone: (519) 746–7616
Orders & donations: 1-888-251-5360
Fax: (519) 746–7617

NEW ZEALAND
Creation Ministries International (NZ)
PO Box 39005
Howick, Auckland 2145

Phone/Fax: (09) 537 4818
A Registered Charitable Trust

SINGAPORE
Creation Ministries International (Singapore)
Clementi Central Post Office
PO Box 195
Singapore 911207

Phone: 9698 4292

SOUTH AFRICA
Creation Ministries International (SA)
PO Box 3349
Durbanville 7551

Phone: (021) 979 0107
Fax: (086) 519 0555

UK & Europe
Creation Ministries International (UK/Europe)
15 Station St,
Whetstone, Leicestershire, LE8 6JS

Phone: 0116-2848-999

USA
Creation Ministries International (USA)
PO Box 350,
Powder Springs, GA 30127

Phone: (800) 616-1264
Fax: (770) 439-9784

OTHER COUNTRIES
Creation Ministries International
PO Box 4545
Eight Mile Plains,
QLD 4113, Australia

Phone: +617 3340 9888
Fax: +617 3340 9889